To Catch an Angel

The sight of the stars makes me dream
- Vincent Van Gogh
- (1823-1890)

Jody Sharpe

Copyright © 2017 Honey Star Publishing
All rights reserved.

ISBN: 1541247256
ISBN 13: 9781541247253
Library of Congress Control Number: 2016913142
CreateSpace Independent Publishing Platform
North Charleston, South Carolina

In Memory of my husband, Steve

Dream Angel

It's after midnight as she dreams of me, her guardian angel. Will she remember the dream she had of me so very long ago? She sleeps on the chaise of her tiny apartment patio near Los Angeles. I whisper," Maggie, it's time. Jeb's spirit will follow."

When she awakens, her heart is full of emotion. The night sky is filled with stars and slow moving clouds. Amid the starry darkness, the twinkly lights of a jet move north. For north is where she will go now. My message is clear. She's waited for the sign from above. In her dream I have called her home to Mystic Bay.

She will go without Jeb, her beloved dog, and Brian, her first love. Losing Jeb then breaking up with Brian has left her despondent and homesick. Yet tonight seeing me in her dream, she has hope for a new beginning. She says her goodnight to God and the sacred sky. She says goodbye to the perfect little life she tried to create, the white picket fenced life never coming to fruition.

At home she will hear again the gentle hum of trees. She always hears them in Mystic Bay. It's her psychic side. She can hear the hum of life in her childhood surroundings, a town known for its psychic angelic ways. The mighty windswept pine in her backyard will hum, whispering its welcome. With Jeb's spirit and me, her guardian angel invisible by her side, dear Maggie Joy Malone will finally come home . . .

1

Madam Norma's Parlor

The cloudy last days of California gloom never bother me. They burn off by afternoon, giving way to blue skies and cotton puff clouds. King, our shepherd mix, and I walk down the steps of the back porch toward the gate. Our blue shuttered house has a small white sign out front with gold lettering that reads, *Madam Norma's Parlor*. A few psychic readings go on weekly there by Gram, and GG, my grandmother and great grandmother. These lovely older ladies are known as the psychic team, Miss Marilyn and Madam Norma. They raised me well with an easy breezy style and plenty of love. It's a peaceful setting, our back yard, our secret garden with its well-mown lawn, birds at the feeder, and bunnies in the bushes. The majestic Bishop Pine with the flowered bench glider near waits for Gram and GG to sip their afternoon tea under its shade. I touch the pine tree I love. I grew up playing in the garden feeling comforted there. I've cried and dreamed so many hopeful dreams, lying on the ground looking up at the tree's magnificence. It was my escape, my dreamy place. I look at the quintessential garden with its hedges and garden jewels, flowering roses, pansies, sweet pea, iris. It's the place where I belong.

Our town is known for its psychics. It is quite the norm here to have a psychic vibe. But I keep my quirky abilities with nature to myself. Only Gram and GG know the extent of my communication with my surroundings. I even water them down when speaking to my dear friend, Jenny. "Was my mother psychic?" I asked GG years ago. "Not at all," my great grandmother replied wistfully. "Your similarities lie in your beautiful face. You are altogether quite different." Then the conversation stopped. How sad, I thought. Gram and GG are so kind. How could my mother's life have ended that way?

Life has a way of taking you places to learn lessons, I ponder, as we walk out the gate to the alley that leads to the side road towards the beach. King's head goes up in the air, his black ears flap back in the breeze. We won't stay long but stand on the crest of a little dune for a moment looking at the sea. Gloom or not, it's a sight to behold; the vast Pacific with boats in the distance and formations of seagulls scouting the sea. Seeing a grandmother walking a baby in a stroller, I think about Gram and GG. Their love almost made me forget my biological mother left me in their arms twenty-six years ago, never to return. Like I was a pair of ill-fitted shoes, she cast me off leaving for Hollywood. Lyla Jasmine, (her stage name) never contacted us. The years I lived in LA, I worried I might run into her. Of course she wouldn't have known me and I didn't comb the hot spots of the rich and famous either. Odd to some, I brush her from my world, trying not to make her absence a big thing in my life. How can I miss someone I don't remember, who never cared about me? I push her out of my mind but if she'd only stay there. And then it comes again, the angst, especially now when I'm home again.

People here know the story of my biological mother, Lyla Jasmine, the pretty Malone girl, born Polly Ann Malone. She left her baby with her mother and grandparents, never to show her face again in the quaint and psychic town of Mystic Bay. People don't gossip here. It's that kind of place. Pushed back in my mind, I try to forget she wouldn't tell them who my father was. Gram and GG wrote persistent letters over several years pleading with her for information, for my sake. She never wrote back. I've wondered about it to obsession; who is my father? Lyla Jasmine catapulted to fleeting fame on the long running TV crime show, *Courtroom 77*. Married to her fourth husband, according to Jenny's love for celebrity gossip, she lives a privileged life in Beverly Hills. She and some unknown man are the reason I'm here in this world, but honestly, all I need are Gram and GG and the stories of my late Great Grandpa Joe. The photos of me as a toddler sitting on his knee are treasures. A good man, he loved his wife and daughter and me. He died when I was four; Gram and GG carried on, saying his spirit was near, keeping us strong. GG sees him sometimes at the end of her bed sending loving thoughts our way. The only memory of him I have is when I smell cigar smoke. "That man loved his cigars almost as much as he loved me," GG says misty-eyed, remembering him. She still keeps in her closet some of the suits he'd wear to court because a hint of cigar still lingers when she opens the closet door. He was the town's country lawyer and he and GG shared an office in the front parlor. Days it was a lawyers' office and nights it was two psychics' parlor. GG kept the sign out front long after he died.

> ***John Joseph Gilbert Attorney at Law***
> ***& Madam Norma's Parlor***
> **20 Moon Road**

"I never knew my mother's father, my Grandfather Sean Malone. His whereabouts are unknown still. He was a philandering traveling salesman with looks like a movie star. He left Gram with my mother, Polly Ann, when she was five. Apparently, he stole Great Grandpa Joe's treasured '57 Chevy and fled. Oh, Great Grandpa Joe got it back all right; Gram still drives it today. Great Grandpa Joe made him sign the divorce papers right then and there or he threatened he'd get his friends in the Mystic Bay Police force to throw him right in jail. "It must be in the genes," GG said of my mother's parting. "She always blamed us her father left. We took her to psychologists, but her anger escalated. She tried to find him to no avail. He had black Irish looks with bright blue eyes, and sweet Gram was smitten. It took her a long time to get over him. But now she has a gentleman caller, as GG calls him. "One marriage is enough," Gram states emphatically, yet she has a lovely romance. They've been together for nearly twenty years now. Mr. Tim Thayer owns the local farmers' market and *Mystic Bay Cheese & Wine*. Both seventy-five, they were in high school together and now share movie and dinner dates on Friday and Saturday nights. I'm glad Gram has someone for her heart clearly breaks at the mention of Polly Ann's departure. She's packed the photos of her away... all but one. It's her high school photo. A fair beauty she was, like Gram's younger photos. I look at it as if a stranger looked like me a bit. History repeated itself when Polly Ann, aka Lyla Jasmine, left me.

"Why did she have me then?" I couldn't help asking them when I was in high school.

GG admitted, "She didn't know she was pregnant until she was far along. We didn't handle it well, Dear. We told her we would raise you so she could continue and go back to college." She went back all right. She never returned. She quit and moved to LA to pursue acting...a thoroughly different life. But I must resemble my father mostly, for my hair is dark and wavy and my skin a deep olive. We concluded he might be from a Spanish background. But where? Who is the mystery man who is my father?

"Let's jog," I urge King. The big bright-eyed black and brown dog has the typical canine loving heart. Loving another dog is therapeutic for me since missing Jeb, my late great golden dog. I rescued Jeb outside a pizza restaurant my sophomore year at UC Davis. He was about six then. Someone in the parking lot was giving him away.

"Whoever wants this pain of a dog can have him," the miserable young man shouted.

"I'll take him," I answered before thinking twice. In college my senior year I lived in a little apartment with Jenny Benfield, not far from Brian's apartment. My grandmother and great grandmother thought Brian was polite enough and never said much, but Jenny was adamant. "No way he's good enough," she'd lecture when I was crying over a forgotten date on his part. "Lose that one, please!" I should have listened but after graduation, I followed Brian to LA to his first job as a law clerk in his uncle's firm like a hug-starved puppy. Jeb came along too. But it was just Jeb and me, as Brian lived a few miles away with his doting hypochondriac mother. He was a total "Mama's boy". That should have been my umpteenth clue our relationship wasn't going to work out. Wasting the years hoping Brian would commit to me was insane. At least during that time I was blessed to have loyal Jeb. I think he really could understand everything that was going on. I'd tell him all my troubles. When Brian and I broke up, Jeb was there for me with as many furry hugs as I needed. Then in a wink he was gone.

Gram and GG rescued King a few weeks before Christmas Eve. That was the day the *July North Show* came to town showcasing my friend Hannah Ryder's book about Mystic Bay called **The Town with the Angel Vibe**. Hannah's ex-boyfriend Sam Blakley had written a novel, **My California Angel**, hinting she and her father were real angels living as humans in California. Hannah and her family were besieged with media; the whole town had a circus-like atmosphere for weeks. Sam Blakley, also Hannah's writing professor, admitted to TV talk show host July North he lied wanting to get Hannah's attention by making people believe she was an angel. Hannah and her dad are, of course, humans like the rest of us mortals.

Subsequently, Hannah wrote a book about the town, how they rallied around her and her family. Her book is about the wonderful changes everyone made after July's TV show revealed Sam's lies. The town worked together imitating angels, doing good works for the benefit of others. There's a big part of the town's Angel Vibe Association (AVA) that rescues animals. So King, cold and hungry and left outside the door of Beachtails' Animal Hospital one night, got lucky and was rescued in the morning by Hannah's vet husband, Josh. Big King now lives happily with us in the town of extraordinary psychic and angel vibes. When I came home last Christmas, King and I bonded big time as I'd just lost my dear Jeb, and Brian, well, he was history. Rescuing here is almost contagious.

Looking to my left before I cross Beach Road, I see him jogging, the same guy I've seen out my window everyday for the past weeks I've been home. Do I know him? I can't see his face, but he looks familiar jogging away with four dogs of various sizes and mixed breeds. He's tall, dark, and handsome, as Gram would say, and a kind soul with a love for animals, but it doesn't take a psychic to see that. The psychic gene was passed down to me; however, just a touch. I can't put out a sign or read futures or tell people about their lives like Gram and GG. The only touch I have is my deep connection to nature, especially when I'm home here in Mystic Bay. I hear a faint hum around every tree, sensing its need for the sea's fog and dew drops in the California morning as they seep into the bark and leaves. When it rains or the sunshine's bright, the trees experience a bliss-like state, loving every breath. They are my lifelines. How do I know this? In this psychic town, it's not uncommon to have abilities like my connection to other living things, like the birds and animals I'm drawn too, even insects. Gram and GG understand me of course, thinking it's an extraordinary ability. But since I've been back, I feel a change. My psychic side seems to have escalated. The tree's hums are more rhythmic, stronger. The deep connection I have is drawing in more experiences, more of nature's connections. Yesterday, as I took a shower, a tiny bird came to flutter in the extra water spraying out the open window. The birds seem to fly closer to me now and the wild bunnies draw nearer too. The colors of the world seem more pronounced. I get almost mesmerized staring at the green trees, the beauty of the sea as it changes colors from dusk to dawn and, oh, the majesty of the sacred nights. I haven't told Gram and GG this yet. I will. I am waiting to see what happens next. For my sixth sense says I'm evolving and it's thrilling.

Yet, having ultra sensitivity has helped in other areas of my life like my career, teaching children with special needs.

I already miss the students I left behind in LA. I hope their new teachers see their potential as I always did.

King and I watch the man with four dogs pick up the two smaller dogs then slowly jog up Bluff Road, then he trots up the hill towards *The Sea Watch Hotel*, the lovely structure recently completed. It overlooks the spectacular Pacific here in Mystic Bay where psychics and angel-like ordinary folk live. Gram said the jogging dog guy most likely is the son of the reclusive author, Marshall Greenstreet The author moved here two years ago with his ailing wife. He spent time here years ago, before I was born, writing his first psychic detective novel in the Connor Diamond series. He interviewed all the towns' famed psychics, including Gram and GG. They say he was so very handsome then, a charmer. When the book became a hit, he gave them a nice monetary gift. A widower now, he is apparently quite ill himself. Gram absolutely loves all of Marshall Greenstreet's Connor Diamond series. The last one published a few years ago, **Diamond's Luck**, sent her into a reading marathon long into the night. Then she started reading all the books in the series again!

The dog jogger out of sight now, King and I sprint across the road towards the beach. I'm going to take him up to Dog Beach and let him run with the wind tomorrow for sure. More seagulls fly overhead. An older gentleman with red tinted sunglasses strolls towards us now. Do I know him? He looks familiar too. He tips his Mystic Bay cap and whistles a tune, the name I seem to forget.

"Pretty dog," he remarks, smiling, and moves on.

"Thank you," I smile back as he walks away south. King turns to look back at him. Everyone is nice here like that whistling man. After Hannah wrote her book about the town even July North caught the town's angel fever, adopted a baby and built a home near the new *Sea Watch Hotel*. I sigh, thinking about my decision to move back. Yes, everything is falling into place now. I'll forget about Brian eventually. Gram, GG and Jenny bet their lives on it. Yet I'll never forget Jeb and the love and comfort he brought me. I'll see him in the precious photos I have and his special place tucked in my heart. Lucky for me, I listened to the angel in my dream. For now, I'll get to see the angelic little faces of the students I'll teach in September, a new job, a new start in the very town I grew up in. I'm babysitting one of my students today, little Emma Rose. I'm volunteering to care for her as needed 'til school starts so her mother Elena can work and go to school. Elena never married Emma Rose's father; she is the sole provider. She is in need of help and volunteering to care for Emma Rose is a privilege.

When we get back, I smell coffee brewing.

"Now Gram, I was going to make the coffee and you keep getting up making it for me!" I kiss my sweet white-haired grandmother who's holding her fluffy white dog, Cookie. The old poodle mix looks comical wearing her little diaper with teddy bears on it. Hannah's husband, Josh, our vet says, "Cookie's just fine except she needs a little extra safety net," a positive way to note her getting on in dog years.

"It's such a happy kitchen," I pet Cookie while surveying the sunny yellow walls freshly painted for my homecoming.

"It's so wonderful having you home, Maggie Joy. I wanted to get up early today and have some time with you before you went to work. To hear you sing around the house again is heaven. We have a nine o'clock client today, early for us. Boy, I bet you're excited about babysitting Emma Rose."

"Actually, Gram, I can't wait. You know I wish I'd never have left Mystic Bay now. What a complete fool I was."

"Oh yes, you should have. You had to find out for yourself if Brian was the right one. No one could tell you what to do."

"I know you and GG didn't think he was good enough, but you're prejudiced."

"Well, Honey, we love you and want you with someone who values you; that's the bottom line."

I feed King and he wolfs down the large portion in five seconds like he usually does. We should put it on YouTube. It could be titled...King Inhales Dinner. Cookie has already eaten like she's a young starving puppy too. Pouring us each a cup, I sit down with Gram at the antique table.

"I made vegetable lasagna last night and put it in the fridge for you and GG. I won't be home till after midnight for sure. Do you want me to bring a couple of pieces of apple torte from Jack's for your lunch on my way to babysit?"

"Well, yes, please but only if you have time and they have extra. We're thrilled that our little cook is here to stay, keeping us company."

"Me, too." I smile listening to her plans for the day, but as she talks my mind strays, glancing around the kitchen where I love to cook while watching the dogs and cat just chilling out. Lost in thought, I visualize my childhood growing up slow within the loving walls of this old house. GG and Great Grandpa Joe built it with love and care for Gram. Then Gram lived with them after her husband left and brought my mother up here too. Then I came along. Strange how the idyllic pattern changed when my Gram's husband left; my grandfather Sean Malone and then my mother left too. Gram tries to hide it, but I know she's beyond hurt; you can see it in her clear blue eyes. She never speaks of my biological mother anymore. She can't go there. I go over and give her a big hug and smile as GG walks in with her walker. She's pretty darn fast. Maybe she really doesn't need it.

"GG, let me help you." I pull the chair out and she sits down. Her snow-white hair catches the light peeking in the window. June gloom is leaving as the month of July moves in. GG's infectious smile warms my heart. At one hundred and counting, she's still an amazing psychic and pretty darn strong. She says the walker is her safety net like flying circus acrobats use, like Cookies' diaper.

"Oh Maggie," GG almost gushes, "It's such a treat having you here again. I can hardly believe it. We don't want you to feel burdened by us. We have Mabel to tend to the housework. But, boy, can we take a breather from her cooking." We all laugh Mabel has been with us for years. She's dedicated and cleans up a storm, though she's not known for her culinary skills. GG doesn't have the stamina anymore to cook and Gram doesn't like to, so Mabel's tasteless meatloaf stuffed with leftover rice mixed-in with long shredded carrots, served with lumpy mashed potatoes is her best dish.

You could lose weight in this house. Her talented husband Acedro is our landscaper and does such an extraordinary job that we're on the local Garden Club's tour every year.

"I'll fatten you two up, GG." I laugh and kiss my great grandmother on the forehead.

"I've got to get ready for work but I've already cooked a lasagna supper. And tomorrow I'm making you the honest to goodness best meatloaf in Mystic Bay, maybe even better than Mabel's, maybe the best in the state." I fix them fried eggs and toast then run upstairs to my room to get ready for my job at *Jack's By The Sea*, the restaurant so near our house I can walk. Stella and Jack Benfield, the owners, and their grown kids, Jenny and her older brother Guy, are great family friends. Jack hired me this summer to make their famous dessert, the apple tortes, and to wait tables on the weekends with Jenny. All during high school I worked there setting tables and helping in the kitchen and waiting tables during vacations, home from college till I met Brian. Guy's son, Patrick, a darling young boy with disabilities, will be one of my students in the fall at Mystic Bay Elementary and is a playmate of Emma Rose.

My clothes are folded neatly in the white whicker drawers and the tiny closet is filled to the max with color coordinated bulging hangers. I pet Blue, our eighteen-year old cross-eyed cat, as he stretches out on the puffy purple comforter. I never know where that cat is looking. His days consist of eating and taking a zillion naps and sometimes I hum a tune and he looks up as if he loves the sound of music. He especially loves it when I sing him to sleep. I wanted to take him with me to college and then LA, but we figured he was safer here. Now that I'm home the cuddling is non-stop. *Who needs a man when an animal sleeps so close? Of course, I know I do.*

When ready, I head downstairs and walk in the parlor where Gram and GG are sitting in twin red leather recliners. Cookie sleeps in her little red bed on the floor, and King wags his tail and sits on the plaid couch looking out the window facing the road. No need for a doorbell. When new clients see a big shepherd mix in the window barking, Gram goes out and coaxes them in. They soon find out that the large dog is just masquerading as a big dog but is really a playful puppy rolling over waiting for pats.

We say our goodbyes. Walking to work down Moon Road to *Jack's By The Sea*, I touch a little tree limb feeling its pulse; it almost sings. The comforting hum of life vibrates around me. It's an amazing thing, isn't it? How lucky I am to have an angel in a dream send me home again.

2

Apple Tortes & Noah's Ark

The misty summer morning with a tease of sun is still cool heading down Moon Road to *Jack's by the Sea*. The seagulls are diving for their breakfast, the tide is out, and rocks form a layer of brown patterns on the sand. The long restaurant with grey shingles and big white sign with a giant fish on it always looks like home to me. A few cars are in the driveway.

The restaurant smells of yummy clam chowder and sour dough bread. As I walk in, Gor Don, the natural clown-like sous-chef greets me with his usual humor, "Ah Maggie, you're the apple of my eye!" Gor Don's mother named him for her two favorite men, Al Gore and Don Knotts. What a combo. He thinks that his name is very cool. Good thing he does. He is working hard and Chef Mario is here for a little while to get things started. He'll come back at four again. He and Jack are bringing in fresh fish with Anthony, the older truck driver. I think Anthony has a crush on me. He smiles a grin with three teeth missing, and I smile back. I'm hoping he's not an example of the kind of guy I'm likely to attract now, older and semi-toothless.

After dating a couple of guys in college proved a joke, I met totally cute Brian through a mutual friend and I was hooked. He was fun, smart and, after law school was heading for LA where his dream job would be waiting.. At first he actually seemed like the real deal and I was impressed. I played down the abilities of my psychic family, never telling him how I heard the hum of life especially in trees in Mystic Bay. Foolish me, moving to Los Angeles to be near him. What was I thinking? Love actually? I found a job right away with high school students with special needs. The kids I loved, but the over-crowded school made it hard to accomplish anything.

I say hello to all, wash my hands, put on the apron, and start slicing apples for the tortes. I make at least twelve tortes a day, sometimes more. Stella's grandma's recipe is a hit with everyone. We serve it warm with vanilla ice cream. I always have a piece if there are leftovers from the night before and bring Gram and GG some. I love it cold with no ice cream and a cup of coffee. I think Stella makes a few extra on the weekends just to give to friends like us.

Tad, the tan and muscular weekend bartender walks in. Why is he here? His white blond hair is slicked back. His green eyes wink at me. He's a surfer with a white shiny toothy smile.

"Tad, hey, how's the surf today?" I say. The attractive guy is my age but seems much younger.

"Epic, Maggie." Then he flips my long brown ponytail. He teases me that I look like an Italian actress, Lianni Giovanni. That's a nice compliment but it makes me wonder about my heritage, where my background comes from, and the father I'll never know.

"Mornin, all you wild and wonderful people," he jokes as he slips his surfer dude body past me. I catch a whiff of coconut sunscreen. It makes me wish for LA, a beach day, and a tan.

"Tad, what's up?" says Jack, as he sets a box of fish on the floor.

"Hey, could I have an advance, Jack?" Tad's always asking for advances. He told us his dysfunctional dad threw him out of the house up in the tony town of Hillsboro for "no good reason." I feel sorry for him because he's a nice guy, yet being nice doesn't solve money problems.

"Sure, Tad," Jack, the pushover says. "But why don't you work a couple extra nights? Then you'll have enough money and won't have to ask." Jack is a big old teddy bear of a man with a smile for everyone.

"Uh, sure, great. When do you need me?"

"Well, tonight and Wednesday are pretty busy lately. Dean is going to leave soon for graduate school, and I could use the help".

"Okay. Tonight I'll be here about five. Hey thanks . . . Bye, beautiful," he says to me as I watch him walk away. I spill some flour on the floor as he leaves. Everyone laughs and I join in, "You know guys, Tad does have puppy dog eyes."

"Yes, I think he has eyes for the lady with the scent of apples," Gor Don kids.

These people make it easy to be myself. I think of Tad's pretty but snooty girlfriend, Missy, a blonde beauty whose family owns a women's clothing boutique in Hillsboro and another one in the Hamptons. Tad says she's from a very wealthy family, was raised in the Big Apple. She comes in here every night he works and sips red wine, making sure none of the female patrons come on to him. Since Tad obviously is one big flirt, she looks each woman up and down as if to say, "Watch it, Sister."

"All the girls like Tad," sings short and stout Mario with his Italian accent. "Why not me? Look at me, I'm a puppy doggie too." Using his index fingers, he pushes his eyes down at the corners to mirror Tad's eyes.

Everyone laughs and Jack kids, "Yes Mario, you are handsome, but if memory serves me, you just got married to Sophia here last month?"

"Yes, of course, I adore Sophia, but all men want to be a little, you know, sexy to all the ladies!"

"Do you want to be, you know, sexy to the ladies, Jack?" Stella kids Jack with a pinch as she walks in. Her laugh is one of those contagious laughs, catching and sunny as she is. I've never seen salt and pepper hair so beautiful. Her beauty has passed down to Jenny. Their eyes are like identical twins, the prettiest chestnut brown.

Jack laughs, "No," as he puts his arms around her waist tied with an apron. "Only you, my little rose petal." Everyone hoots and whistles.

Jenny walks in, her long blonde hair tied in a ponytail too. "Hey everybody, what's so funny?"

"How about Anthony, the handsome fish man for Maggie?" Mario kids me now.

"Stop it, Mario. I'm too young for him. He's like sixty!"

Everyone laughs at me. I've known them all since I was a little girl and so I'm the one who laughs the hardest.

"We've got to find someone great for Maggie," Jenny says with her arm around my shoulder. "Jason and I are looking for just the right guy this time," she whispers to me.

Jenny and Stella are going to look for wedding dresses in San Francisco today. Since the end with Brian, Jenny and her fiancé Jason Doherty are trying to fix me up. Last weekend's blind date flopped big time. Jason manages his dad's tree farm, Phil's Christmas Trees, and this guy, Lance, is their accountant. He's very good looking and a math whiz, but with zero personality. Math whiz, I'm not, and so the double date ended like a comedy sitcom. He started apotheosizing how math is the language of the universe and I almost fell asleep, my head in the pepperoni pizza. Then Jason shared with him, much to my chagrin, my Great Grandmother and Grandmother's talents as the town's best-known psychics. Then he had to, of course, explain to him that I'm a wee bit psychic too. He made up a story that I could predict Lance's future looking into his eyes. Suddenly, poor Lance didn't feel well and left Bob's Pizza fast as lightening. We laughed and ate the pizza he didn't eat. Why waste Bob's best pepperoni? We'll laugh for eternity about that disaster. If I'd told Lance I heard trees hum he might have fainted dead away.

After all the tortes are in the oven and five are out cooling, Stella asks me, "Maggie dear, on your way out could you take half a torte to Madam Norma and Marilyn and half to Elena and Emma Rose? Wait till you meet that precious child. She and Patrick have such fun. You will be such a fine teacher for them both." Stella hugs me.

"Thanks for the confidence. I can't wait for school to start and wow, thanks for the tortes. Do you have enough though for tonight?"

"Every time you're here I want you to take some okay? You're such a help to us. Jenny is so thrilled you're home and working here...and the wedding next month and you maid of honor. I can't wait for you to pick out your dress if we can find that color. If not, I'll have it made!" Stella is so excited and it's fun to see it all happening. I can't wait.

As the only attendant, Jen said I could choose anything as long as it's shocking pink. I've looked in all the bride's magazines we can find to no avail. After thanking Stella, I cleaned up my station.

This is a great job to make ends meet. Jack wants me to continue to wait tables on weekends when school starts. My dream job is really happening. Plus Jenny teaches fifth grade there too. And me? Just seven kids in a classroom, a job offered almost like magic from an innovative grant for the Mystic Bay Elementary School. My last job was so stressful and my relationship with Brian was so done. Then to have to live without Jeb was too much. But now I have a new beginning. I pick up the torte ready to leave when Stella says, "Oh, on your way, would you have time to take a torte up Bluff Road to Marshall Greenstreet and his son Noah?"

"Sure, which house do they live in?" *Well now, I just might get to meet the dog jogger! This should be interesting.*

"You go up Bluff Road below The Sea Watch Hotel and turn on Sea Watch Drive. Marshall has been so ill since his wife died. I take one up every two weeks but today I have to shop!" Stella continues as she walks out the door, "It's the modern gray block and glass...they live next to July North's new stone and white-shuttered house. You can't miss it. The Greenstreet house has wrought iron gates that only close at night and the lawn has lots of statues of angels and animals. It's quite a menagerie but somehow so serene. Thank you so much, dear."

"I'm on my way." I take the two tortes and walk home. I set them on the table. Since they're big, I cut one in half and leave half out for Gram and GG and put the other half in a little basket for Elena and Emma Rose. I put the whole one for the Greenstreet's in a pretty basket and tie it with a blue ribbon. Gram and GG are in the backyard sitting in the bench glider watching the birds and bunnies and the bright blue sky. The lawn sprinkler waves back and forth, filtering golden sunlight. Cookie is napping, snoring really, on Gram's lap, and King's head rests on GG's lap as usual, ignoring the bunnies. He's a lap dog, or at least, his head is. He sees me, gets up, and runs to me. As I kneel down to hug him, a bee buzzes near. But something's peculiar. It has feathery golden wings, and I can't recall ever seeing one like that before. I watch it fly away.

"Hi ladies," I brought you half the famous apple torte from Stella. I'm taking the other half to Elena and Emma Rose."

"Oh, that's so sweet; our lunch today. I'll call Stella and thank her later. You will fatten us up for sure, dear," Gram remarks.

I get up and tease them with a wink, "Oh, and by the way, I'm taking a torte up to Marshall Greenstreet and his son, Noah."

GG sighs, "Oh, how wonderful. Please remember us to Marshall." Before I can answer, she continues, "I have a feeling about Noah, Maggie. You are going to like him!" GG is teasing me back and takes my hand. "He's handsome and kind."

I roll my eyes. "Okay, GG, start planning. A Dog Beach wedding sounds good."

Gram shakes her head. "You deserve someone more thoughtful than Mama's Sonny Boy." Our smiles grow into laughter. Brian's mom used to call him her Sonny Boy. I think, *which one of us was the biggest loser?*

GG, reading my mind like she can at odd times pipes in, "He's the loser and you know it." Yes, she can really read minds upon occasion.

"Oh, GG," I say, kissing her on the top of her head. "You're so right." We say goodbye and I get in my yellow mustang and head up Bluff Road, feeling a little pang in my heart. I thought Brian was the one, that my college romance would be the fairytale kind. But once I moved to LA, it became a fractured fairy tale. Then Jeb passed away, and I went home for Christmas, without Jeb, without Brian, without hope.

The scenic road almost commands me to stop and stare mesmerized by the rolling ocean. It seems to go on for forever. The Sea Watch Hotel stands like a castle on the tip of the bluff. Dotted below is an array of new custom built houses. Turning onto the winding road before the hotel sign, I pass a few lovely homes, including the inviting stone house with white shutters that must be July North's. There is a star-shaped plaque on the gate that reads, "Northstar". Next door to it, are the lacy wrought iron gates open to a yard full of angels and animal statues held in a beautifully manicured yard. The modern home is spectacularly built with large windows reaching to the roof. The gate also has a plaque on it, "Josephine's Garden."

I maneuver up the drive nervously because I'll get to meet the very man who has intrigued me each morning these last few weeks. I hear the dogs barking in the back yard. Maybe I'll only get to meet his father. I get out smoothing my favorite sweater, the red polka dot one, and I touch my hair, making sure the ponytail is in place. Another golden-feathered winged bee lands on my side view mirror. I'm captivated for a moment. It flies away. The trees on the Greenstreet property hum almost like a kitten's purr. Finally centered, picking up the torte neatly placed in the basket, I walk up the stone steps and ring the doorbell. More barking ensues, this time from within.

A man opens the door and I almost drop the pretty basket.

"Hello," he says kindly. He is gorgeous up close, even with thick black-rimmed glasses. With a beaming smile he says, "You must be Maggie from the restaurant."

Noah Greenstreet, thirtyish, has dark hair, and jeweled amber eyes. His body looks like that of a Greek god. He wears jeans and a white tee shirt. His smile is perfect. I gulp, can't speak. He takes off his glasses.

"Can't see with these, only need them when I write," he smiles again. "I'm Noah Greenstreet and you are Maggie, aren't you?"

I've seen this guy before, but where? Noah Greenstreet's eyebrows lift, waiting for an answer.

"Yes, Maggie Malone, that's me."

"Have we met before?" He seems perplexed.

"Uh, no, I don't think so." That's all I can say. No doubt I've a strange expression on my face. It's all I've got. Then I hear an older man's voice.

"Who's at the door, Josephine darling?"

Noah's expression changes to a sad one.

"Dad, it's a young lady bringing us an apple torte." He turns back to me with a smile that could light up a gloomy night.

"You have no idea how addicted to apple tortes my Dad and I are now. Stella and Jack are spoiling us rotten. Thank you for bringing it, Maggie."

Four dogs rush up from the hall but all stop short when Noah commands them. One large shepherd mix, two of them small, and one is a beautiful Yellow Lab. They wag their tails then sit down as if trained by an expert.

"They won't hurt you. I've rescued three in the year I've lived here. That's Smarty, Dad's Lab he rescued a couple of years ago. The others are Shadow, Murphy and Nursie. She's little but she's the nurse to them all. I brought them home a few months ago. Hannah and Josh Ryder found them abandoned in a warehouse in San Francisco. Look at these guys!" He pets Smarty, then looks at me and I hand him the basket.

Shadow is a cuddly and looks like King. Murphy and Nursie are darling smaller black and white mixes.

"Pretty dogs," I say almost tongue-tied, imitating the whistling man I met this morning on the walk.

"Well, no one has ever said that." Noah laughs again. "They bring lots of joy. Hey, by any chance, is Joy your middle name?"

My mouth wants to move but can't for a moment, then I blurt out, "Yes, how did you know that?"

"I'm sorry. I'm a little psychic or I've got some psychicness, I call it. I've had it all my life and it's escalated a bit since I moved here to help Dad. I didn't mean to scare you." Noah looks worried.

"Oh, I don't mind. Lots of people are psychics here, you know." There is a short pause and since I'm unsettled because he knew my middle name I blurt out, " Well, my grandmother and great-grandmother give their regards to your father. He interviewed them back when he wrote **One Psychic Summer**. They're, you know, psychic too."

Noah seems surprised. " Wow, how nice. Please tell them hello. I'd love to meet them sometime."

" Well, I better go." I turn to leave, turning the wrong way away from the car.

"Oops," I smile and turn the right way...stuck...want to leave but wait for him to say something again.

"Thank you, Maggie. I'd invite you in, but Dad's kind of a handful today. His caregivers have the day off, but please thank the Benfield's for me. Tell Stella and Jack I will be down soon to get dinner for Dad and me. You're all pretty special here in this town. No wonder my parents moved here. And you, Maggie, are especially sweet to bring it today with your busy schedule."

"You're welcome." I head for the car, almost tripping on nothing. As I get in, Noah and the dogs are still at the door watching me. I smile and give a quick wave. Looking in the rear view mirror I see Noah's waving too. Oh God, why do I always get nervous around good-looking men? It was like that with Brian; I was never my true self. He didn't like my hinting I had psychic abilities too. He thought Gram and GG were strange and the town was off-kilter. "Psycho," he said. What did I see in him anyway? Maybe I was escaping my past, leaving for LA, away from the town where my mother grew up. But I moved to LA and she lived there too. A psychologist might have a few deductions about that. Maybe I should make an appointment with one? Living there chasing the dream of him was a learning experience. Now being back home brings me joy again. Joy! Noah knew my name was Joy and he knew I had a busy schedule? Amazing! I drive out the driveway down Bluff Road, thinking about his dad's psychic character, Connor Diamond, in the series Gram talks about. I never read the books. I don't remember where I met Noah Greenstreet but I hope he didn't guess what I was thinking. Our paths must have crossed. His face is too familiar. His smile is a smile I've seen somewhere. He even asked me if we'd met. I rack my brain, but the memory wouldn't come. He's one good-looking man, Mr. Noah Greenstreet, jogger, animal lover, and psychic.

3

An Angel And A Rose

"Thank you, Maggie," the dark-haired beauty Elena Torres says, getting into her car. "I don't know what I'd do without you or Sharon Manuel helping me like this."

"It's my pleasure, Elena. She'll be fine with me today. She seemed to take to me right away. We are going for a picnic, aren't we?" Emma Rose nods. Thankfully she's not afraid meeting me the first time. She knows I will be her new teacher and she has taken my hand. After waving Elena goodbye, my little five year old charge and I look down at her orange cat, Princess, winding herself around Emma Rose's legs. "Sweet little cat you have," I say. Emma

Rose smiles; her dark hair is in a ponytail like mine and her smile is heavenly.

"Want to have a picnic?" Elena prepared a little basket of peanut butter and jelly sandwiches cut out in the shape of hearts, little fruit drink boxes, and sliced apples. She nods, so off we go. Elena rents Stella and Jack's house on Meadowbrook Lane off Sea Breeze Drive, just before the acres of bigger ranches and farms. Behind each small ranch house on the street are deep back yards with a sliver of a stream running through. It's beautiful now with the leaves moving in a light breeze, shining in the afternoon sun, and the cool summer air just right for a walk. The trees hum low; their perfect reflections look back at us from the water. The flowers dance in the wind just like Emma Rose's eyes. I set out the small plastic tablecloth I brought. As we sit down, I take the picnic things out. Emma Rose is delighted as she takes a few bites. Famished, I almost swallow mine whole. I keep thinking about Noah but know I have to concentrate on Emma Rose.

There is a little brass plaque at the edge of the property on the path to the stream. I've seen its saying before and it's a favorite of mine so I read it to Emma Rose.

> **A Kiss from the sun for pardon**
> **The song of the bird for mirth**
> **One's nearer to God in a garden**
> **Than anywhere else on earth**

I talk awhile as we eat, telling her about the birds that fly by, the bubbling brook and pretty trees, and about school in a few months, and how much fun we'll have with Patrick and the other kids. We finish our little lunch and I pack it up. As we get up, I see him about twenty feet away. I drop the picnic things on the ground and rub my eyes. It's Jeb, my golden dog, sitting, panting just like he used to while he waited for me to take our walks. He's young again, a happy glint in his brown eyes as real as day. Stunned, I can't say anything. Then he turns and moves east up along the stream. In silence I take Emma Rose's hand and we follow. Then in a flash he disappears. I can hardly breathe for I've just seen the spirit of my beloved dog. Emma Rose points. Did she see him too? No, she's pointing to a black bird on the path, a dead bird. We walk up to it, but something strange happens. The bird moves, lifting up as if someone is holding it and with each second it begins to stretch its wings, becoming more alive. Then, as if tossed gently in the air, it flies away.

Emma Rose points again. "Angel," she says with a smile. I turn to look at her and get down on my knees to her eye level.

"What did you say?" She doesn't speak again.

"Did you say angel?"

She is still pointing, nodding and smiling at the sky where the bird flew away.

"Did you see a dog?"

She shakes her head no. How can this be? I turn around and stand up. Am I daydreaming? Did I really see Jeb? The angel in my dream said Jeb's spirit would come with me to Mystic Bay. But did Emma Rose actually see an angel save a fallen bird? Jeb has been dead for months and Emma Rose, the little girl with Down's Syndrome, has always been mute."

4
Angels Calling

It's way after midnight when I return home. King is lying on his dog bed beside GG's brass bed. He lies beside her each night, and it's a beautiful thing. I look in on Gram. She's in her powder blue bedroom with the light still on, the book she's reading on her chest, her glasses still on her nose. Cookie snuggles next to her, her head on the other pillow. I gently take her glasses, placing the book on the nightstand. It's an older novel, **Diamond's Fury**, by Marshall Greenstreet. I turn out the light. She doesn't stir. I make sure the nightlight is on in the bathroom then head out in to the chilly night to lie on the chaise and watch the moon glow. The swirling clouds with the moon behind them light the star-filled chilly night. King comes out the doggie door to be with me till I go upstairs myself. He does this every night. Then back he goes to be with GG.

"How was your day, boy? Did you help Gram and GG with their psychic readings?"

Of course he doesn't answer. How I wish he could.

"Can you see angels?" King sits and puts his left paw up for shaking.

"Good boy, you're a southpaw just like me." I shake his paw and rub behind his ears. I review the astonishing day and tell King all about it.

"Noah Greenstreet, a handsome and psychic man, asked me if we'd met before. How surreal, but where? College? LA? Did he grow up here? No, I'd remember that. I do remember him too...it's so weird, King. And today, did Emma Rose see an angel or just a sick bird regain strength, then fly away? Elena told me she's never spoken a word, but I swear she said 'Angel.' And was Jeb by the stream? What's happening to me? "

I close my eyes. King puts his head on my lap. Not alarming Elena was my priority; should I tell her? What if I was hallucinating, hoping to see Jeb, thinking of angels? Yawning, I announce to my companion, "It's time to say goodnight to God and the moon."

King and I walk back in the house and he turns to look at me like he did at the whistling man today. "Goodnight boy," I whisper. I climb the stairs and get ready for bed. Blue, snug on the comforter again, opens one eye and is gone. I get in my bed, exhausted. A long white feather sits on my bedside table. Picking it up, admiring its perfect beauty, I wonder where it came from. Maybe Gram put it there because GG can't walk up the stairs anymore. Mabel was here today so perhaps she found it. Wrapping around today's events, I'm trying to make sense of it all. Analyzing it has exhausted me. As Blue purrs next to me, my eyes finally close in prayer. "God, did Jeb lead us to an angel? Did Emma Rose see one?" Fading now, inevitable dreamland comes, taking me away to parts unknown.

Noah is jogging up Beach Road. I've waited at my window till I see him pass and jog up towards his home with dogs in tow before King and I set out. Why am I afraid to run into him? July North had a show about daddy-less girls having trouble in relationships with men. With little or no self-esteem, they have to learn self-worth without a father figure. It's true if I look at my relationship with Brian. I let him walk all over me. We did everything he wanted. I even moved away from the place I loved and needed for my soul, away from Gram and GG who were getting old. They are my mothers and keep me feeling loved, wanted, and valued.

No, I won't be afraid. Tomorrow, I'll go out about the time I usually see him. I'll have more confidence. "Right Blue?" Blue looks at me with crossed-eyed interest. As I finish getting on my jogging clothes, I whisper a song for him he likes, an old song Gram and GG sing around the house. Tiptoeing down the stairs with Blue carefully stepping down each step in anticipation of his breakfast, I arrive in the kitchen to get the coffee brewing since no one is stirring. When King and I go out to the yard I almost stumble. Clearly, I have to find out what really happened with Emma Rose. Trying to process it all, the angel sighting, and seeing Jeb, I know I must tell Gram and GG about it when they wake up. King and I walk the whole way to Dog Beach. On the way I pass the whistling man again wearing his Mystic Bay cap and tinted glasses. "I love your whistling," I say to him.

He stops with a big smile. "Why, thank you. I hope you don't mind a pretty tune, dear." He takes a moment to bend down to pet King. "Hello again."

"Excuse me sir, but have we met? I'm Maggie and this is King."

The man smiles, "Nice to meet you. I'm new in town, name's Neal Beasley. Well, goodbye, Maggie and King. Have a nice day." He tips his hat and moves on. King turns to look at him again.

Dog Beach sparkles with life as the various shapes and sizes of dogs leap in the waves and run down the sand. King is partial to big waves and runs right in. I see my high school friend, Hannah and her husband, Josh Ryder and their little darling ginger baby twins in a stroller. "Ginger babies," GG calls the little red heads, just like their mom. Their dogs and pet deer, Dawn, run in pure delight. Hannah rescued the dwarfed deer when it was a fawn. Hannah and Josh are a beautiful couple. The great thing is they are both such nice people. We say hello and Hannah asks how my move went and when we can get together for lunch. "Anytime, give me a call," I tell her. She puts my new number into her phone. I notice how Josh and Hannah's blue eyes sparkle golden like sunshine on the sea.

We say our goodbyes and I watch Josh kiss them all. "Say hello to Madam Norma and Miss Marilyn," Josh calls as Hannah strolls off to her truck and Josh walks to his vet hospital.

I wave and think that maybe I'll ask Hannah about seeing angels. Maybe she saw them as a child as Emma Rose did. Perhaps that's why she wrote the angel stories that Sam Blakley turned into the novel. No, I can't ask her. It would be unkind to bring it up. It was a painful time for her then, but now her life seems idyllic. She went through tremendous pain as a child when her mother died suddenly in a car accident. "Sadness is just a part of life," GG always says. "But the blessed parts are what keeps us going."

How nice to have a family life like Hannah and Josh someday. Maybe I should call Brian. What a pathetic idea. "Forget him," my mind yells. King comes back when I call him, as happy as a clam, another Gram expression.. As we walk home, I look for the man I call whistler. He's nowhere. I look up Bluff Road for a sign of Noah. How I wish I'd left earlier so I could've run into him. We walk home, but Gram and GG are still asleep as I leave for work.

The apple tortes are in full speed now, the last in the oven. I'm cleaning my workspace when Nancy and Edie, the comical owners of the best cleaning service in town, Mystic Maids, come into the kitchen. Greatly excited, with pink vacuum in hand, Nancy says in her husky voice, "There's a **very** handsome man here to see you, Maggie."

Edie almost shouts, "He's hunk-a-licious. Girl! Go out there **now**!" She takes her pink plastic-gloved hands and pushes me out into the hall and up to the entryway of the restaurant. I look back and hear the crew whistling and Gor Don cat-calling in the kitchen. Nancy says in a loud voice with dry humor, "What you gotta do to get a man like that? Look like her?" Edie shouts back an elongated version of "Ye-e-s -s."

Of course, Murphy's Law or Malone's Law, there stands Noah Greenstreet in his faded jeans and a forest green tee shirt. He's more handsome than I remember. I wipe a piece of unruly hair out of my eyes and face. "Hello, Maggie. It's good to see you again. And if you don't mind," Noah takes his fingers and touches my face. I jump back. "I'm sorry, you had flour there." He laughs, and I wipe my face with my apron.

"That's okay, thanks." I'm embarrassed again.

"I brought your basket back; thank you again." I nod. Noah hesitates then says, "I'd like to take you to dinner tonight or any night if you're free. . . unless you're engaged or something? You're not, right? My psychicness tells me."

I'm shocked as I stare at Noah Greenstreet. How did he guess I didn't have a boyfriend? Maybe it's written all over my flour-filled face. Should I go out with him? I've never gone out with such a gorgeous looking man, let alone a psychic one. I blurt out fast, "No, I'm not, I mean, yes, I'm free tonight. I live at 20 Moon Road; the sign out front says Madam Norma's Parlor. " Oh, God, I'm babbling.

Noah's elated, "Oh, I know the house. Okay, great... tonight? Early? Five okay? I want to take you for a walk down Main Street so you can show me this special town, then we'll go to the prettiest place I know for dinner." I nod and he says with a grin, "I'll look forward to it all day." Gorgeous, psychic Noah makes me quiver. We say goodbye while I shake like a cavewoman without fur on a wintry day.

I touch my apron, reminiscent of Cinderella going to the ball. What will I wear? The razzing when I get back in the kitchen is loud. "Maggie's in love," sings Mario in a pretty convincing fake operatic voice. Nancy and Edie start singing, "She's In Love With The Boy" as Gor Don takes my hand and turns me around in a two-step twirl.

In a daze when I get home, I tell Gram and GG about the date with Noah and how he's a psychic too. They are elated, like the chattering mice and birds in Cinderella. At the speed of an elderly bird with a walker, GG goes to find a necklace. Gram insists I wear my turquoise sweater because it goes with my eyes. GG's Hawaiian pearl necklace is perfect for me to wear. She insists I keep it. Great Grandpa Joe gave it to her on their wedding day.

"GG, it's only a first date," I manage to squeak out. King runs around excited too, but ole Cookie keeps on dreaming. I make a turkey meat loaf, put it in the oven, and then take a shower, still not believing this is really happening. He didn't even say where we're going. I fumble with the soap and almost slip on the suds. I'm behaving like a teenager. "Stop it." As I towel dry, I hear my cell ring. Is he canceling? No, he doesn't even know my cell number. I answer it. It's Elena.

Elena is crying. "Maggie, today Emma Rose said "Angel," did you teach her to talk?" She cries again into the phone.

I try to explain, "Elena, Emma Rose said it yesterday, but I thought I was hearing things. She only said it once." I explain the situation as it happened, my late dog's appearance, the dead bird, everything. "I'm sorry, I should have told you, but it was all so fantastic, I couldn't believe it was real. You told me she doesn't talk."

"Never before." Elena cries. "It's a miracle!" We make a plan. Elena will come over tomorrow with Emma Rose to meet with Gram, GG, and me. She also wants to bring Reverend Carlos Manuel and his wife Sharon, who babysits Emma Rose as well.

As I share the news with Gram and GG, their wise faces tell me they're not surprised. Gram is wide-eyed looking at GG, "Mother, you said something beautiful was coming, something good. Was this it? "

GG gazes out the window as if transfixed on a place far away. "Oh yes, Marilyn, dear. This is what I saw in my dreams, something good coming to Mystic Bay. And of course, it was the angels. The angels are calling!"

5

Moon Bathing

It is a tiny bit awkward at first, Noah at the door and Gram and GG sizing him up with psychic vibes. But Noah is charming and polite. After a walk around town, he's taking me to the Sea Watch Hotel's new restaurant, The Starfish Grill. It's Wednesday so it's the very popular, "Summer Nights On Main." All the stores have open house till nine p.m. There are inviting sales, and they serve coffee, tea and cold drinks.. It's a night to meet and greet the townsfolk and tourists. Gram chatters on and on how she loves The Connor Diamond series, and how absolutely charming his dad was when he interviewed the psychics in town for his first novel. "I can't wait for his new book, Noah. But we heard your father is ill? Can we help somehow?"

"It's not a known fact, though we are putting a press release out tomorrow. My Dad is suffering from dementia. I finished his novel for him from his notes. You are the first people I've told that aren't working with me." Noah looks down, a shadow of sadness crossing his handsome face. Gram places her hand on his arm in a motherly way. "We're so sorry dear," she utters softly.

"We wish him well," GG adds and I notice tears in her eyes, for she always spoke so highly of him.

He expresses his appreciation for their kindness and we say our goodbyes. Noah lightens up as we walk over to Main Street, bright with geraniums and sweet alyssum hanging on the red brick and stucco buildings. Some have shutters painted with antique charm. I've put on sandals for the walk, leaving my heels in Noah's car. He's "dressed to the nines" as GG always says when a man looks like he walked out of a magazine shoot. He wears khakis and a blue plaid button down shirt with a navy jacket. I point out the stores and describe each business owner, introducing him to everyone I can. Walking on the west side of the street, we see sandy-haired Andy Walin and Mary Jo, his pretty wife, at the door of his families' Wizard Wrench Hardware. Andy's dad, Willie, is the long time mayor and a Palmist. Andy and his mother Alma have psychic abilities too. Alma does Reiki, and Andy is training with his Palmist father. He and Mary Jo organize The Angel Vibe Association called AVA animal rescues in town. They're going to dog sit for Noah while he's away.

Andy's dad, Willie read my palm once and said I'd have three children. Where are they, I wonder? Just stars in my eyes, I guess. We poke our heads into most of the stores and Noah meets as many folks as I know at Mystical Me Bakery, Nita and Art's Quaint Shop, and Olson's Books. Then we head toward the *Next Door Café*. I'm tour guiding, explaining everything I can cram in about the town. Laurjean Whitefeather, the owner of *Next Door Café*, is just leaving the town's favorite restaurant with her cute little boy, Stevie. Once a week the town opens late for Summer Nights on Main and Laurjean says they've got to be open just like everybody else even though they're open for breakfast and lunch only. Tonight they serve dessert, their colossal hot fudge sundaes.

"Laurjean and Stevie Whitefeather, this is Noah Greenstreet." Laurjean and Noah shake hands. With great flair, a single green pen holds her abundance of silvery hair in a twist. She wears an apple green jumper and green flats. Stevie is shy but shakes Noah's hand. Laurjean and Donnie decided to foster and adopt the little boy after Hannah's book came out. He's doing well and loves to help his father in the kitchen and Mom with setting tables.

"Why, sure as I'm standing here, Noah, you've been here awhile and you haven't been over to our restaurant. Come on in, anytime. It'll be on us. You bring pretty Maggie in and sky's the limit. Okay?"

"I sure will, Laurjean, thank you. Maggie says you have the best breakfast and lunches in town." Laurjean admits he's correct and Stevie says, "My Dad makes the giant BLT." Noah tells him he definitely is going to order the giant BLT when he comes in. "My hubby is as toasty as his BLT's now that he's retired, working with me and Chris, our older son." Away they go with a goodbye and a wave, off to see Hannah and Josh's pet deer who's holding court at Dear Dogs, Etc. tonight. Above The Next Door Café is Katie's Cottage, a vintage clothing shop owned by Katie, Chris' girlfriend, and her Mom. Our minister Reverend Carlos walks down Main toward us. After I've introduced them and he moves on, I relay that Reverend Carlos' wife, Sharon, is a medium and babysits Emma Rose too.

Noah says out of earshot, "Wow, it seems there are a lot of psychics here in town. How many would you guess?" I have to think a bit before answering.

"Um...it's hard to tell. I doubt anyone's counting. Years ago doing his research, your dad must have heard that Mystic Bay has a reputation as the most largely populated psychic California town around. Maybe it's in the water, the air."

"It seems to be."

We move along past the Old Post Office with its bell tower. It chimes from nine a.m. to six p.m. each day. The soothing sound is one of the many comforting aspects of this seaside haven. Coming out of the police station is big Jim Nero, the new police chief, and his photographer wife Sue. I make the introductions. Big Jim's taken over since Donnie, Laurjean's husband, retired. Donnie works full time at the Café now. Sue looks at Noah, "I had the pleasure of meeting your father when he moved here and I was wondering if you two would be interested in collaborating with me on a book I want to publish with photos and stories of the rescue animals in town? You know our psychic town is now known for it's volunteering ways and I'd love to talk to you both about it. Other than our expenses, the money made could go to our AVA here in town." Noah graciously imparts the information about his father, but insists he is more than willing to discuss the book.

" I'd be delighted to work with you. We have five rescue dogs at our house now." He and Sue make a date to meet at *The Next Door Café* for lunch.

We walk across the street to the Town Square with its grand bandstand and statue of our Mayor Willie. We move our way back down Main Street to the newly opened Café Nikos. Known for it's delicious coffees and desserts, it's becoming more popular than the biggest store chain, Star Coffee, located in Riverton, the next town over. Next we decide to stop in at Tarot & Tea to see Tina Beaujolais, Jason's mom, who isn't there. His Grandma Ethel Marie is totally engaged with a tourist reading tarot cards at a little table in the back. Jenny is working tonight for Tina. I introduce Noah to her. I can tell they like each other right away. Jason's tiny little Grandma Ethel Marie and her daughter Tina own the charming shop of teas and teapots and cups from around the world. She barely looks up, calling out, "Come in for a free reading." Ethel Marie is reading for the tourist who's so enthralled with the cards, she doesn't look up either. Jenny says Jason and his mother and dad are shopping in San Francisco tonight for shirts and jackets to wear at the beach wedding. As we leave the store, I tell Noah that he'll like Jason just as much as he likes Jenny.

Noah remarks, "She's sweet. You know I met Jason and his dad when I bought a Christmas tree at their farm last year. Isn't his last name Doherty, though?"

"Yes, his mom and dad never married but are still a couple. Jason's taken over the Christmas Tree Farm and is doing a great job."

"By the way, I watched *The July North Show* from home when it was held here Christmas Eve. I was amazed how Hannah and Josh turned the mayhem around with her book. I know July and her sister January who are my new next-door neighbors. July introduced me to Hannah and Josh after the show aired and they told me about the dogs they'd found at the warehouse. Andy and Mary Jo Walin were fostering them... interesting how it all came together for good."

"You know, it happens all the time here, everyday in fact." I don't tell him about Emma Rose. I really witnessed it for sure, but it still feels like a dream.

At the end of Main, we pass Hannah out front of Dear Dogs Etc. Dawn, the dwarfed fawn, is on a leash and some kids have gathered, including Stevie with Laurjean. The pink and green shop with pet gifts galore is a happy meeting place for humans and their furry friends. We chat for a while and Noah seems charmed by everyone's friendliness and the darling deer that behaves like a dog. The clock tower chimes seven. We walk back to the house and drive up Bluff Road to the hotel. Noah's barely gone into town the year he's been staying with his father and finishing his last novel. Now he acts like he has warm impressions in sync with mine. As we drive, I gaze at the pewter tinted ocean, thinking of Jeb and the angel appearing to Emma Rose and how they will undoubtedly change everything now. The angel in my dream said Jeb's spirit would follow me. Did he know I'd witness the little girl's vision? I turn to look at Noah and he glances at me, smiling. He turns into the long drive of the hotel.

"Something's up, am I correct? Something amazing?"

I'm stunned and wait a beat before I answer.

"Something amazing did happen yesterday. Wow, you really are psychic aren't you? I haven't told anyone but Gram and GG and I don't know if I should."

"You can tell me anything. Mother taught me always to keep secrets."

Thankfully, the conversation stops as we arrive at the hotel and the valet takes the car. I'd like to tell him but should I? And of course, I'm wondering where I've met this man who seems so familiar to me. My psychic abilities are becoming more pronounced here, but Noah says his are too. But is it really so far out to think that in a town with such a psychic and angel connection that angels could appear and dog spirits could really visit the ones they loved?

The Sea Watch Hotel is finished with California breezy and comfortable style. Finally seated in a sea green leather booth in the corner of the solid glass-walled restaurant, we watch a perfect sun set a golden shine on the dark water. I sigh and take a sip of Chardonnay.

"Well, Maggie Joy." Noah says in a soft voice. "I'd love to hear what happened yesterday. I'm intrigued. Maybe I can help somehow? I promise I won't tell a soul." He looks so sincere; kindness radiates in an aura around him. Momentarily, I'm unable to speak.

"Maggie, please tell me what's happened, especially since it seems we've met before. My gut instinct says it's wondrous, that I'm supposed to know."

The aura is gone and my composure returns. My intuition tells me to explain even though we're newly acquainted.

"These past two days have been extraordinary, really." As I impart the information about Jeb's appearance, Noah's eyes widen. When I tell him little Emma Rose was thought to be mute, yet she blurted out "Angel" he shakes his head in disbelief. Then I include how GG knew something beautiful was coming, that angels were calling us. What I don't say is, this is déjà vu. We've met like this somewhere. I know him. Noah waits a moment or two, processing it all. He takes my hand in his. His amber eyes glisten.

"This is indeed a miracle. I've always believed in angels myself. This town, known for its acts of kindness, now has a child seeing angels and speaking her first word! This is awesome! Before I moved here, I never gave much thought to rescuing animals; neither did Dad. I never gave a thought about volunteering in the past and now I'm driven to do good works here, help with the book Sue Nero talked about, and maybe, when the time is right, even write Emma Rose's story." Noah looks out at the sun's last rays dipping away into the ocean. Then he turns to me again, "I want to hear about your dog, Jeb!"

"Noah. Please wait to write anything until we know what we're going to do after we meet Elena tomorrow." I normally would be angry with myself for telling him, yet my heart knows he needed to know. The story of Jeb and our bond was easy to tell. Of course I leave Brian's name out of the story, referring to it as my move to LA with my ex-boyfriend. But I do tell him about the angel in my dream, how he told me to move home, that Jeb's spirit would follow. As the sun finishes setting, Noah and I look out at the giant spotlights that have turned on, lighting the sea, waves tumbling up the rocky cliffs. He reaches for both my hands.

"An angel in a dream? How beautiful, Maggie. How wonderful you saw Jeb again and then Emma Rose saw an angel and you were there to witness it all. It's a miracle! I believe our animal companions are earth's angels. I can't believe I never saw it before. That's what I want to write about someday. And now you have King and Cookie and your cat... there are always animals to find and love."

My worry seems to calm and I feel comforted by his words. We order dinner, but I'd really rather just stare at him. Noah is vegetarian and the Star Fish Grill's vegetarian ravioli doesn't disappoint us. We discuss the novel, claiming that Hannah and her Dad are angels; thus the pathetic confession of the author on *The July North Show*. Noah's savvy and kind, famous neighbor, July told him that the blessings coming out of Hannah's publishing of her own book, **The Town With the Angel Vibe**, are one thousand fold. People are doing good works every day.

Noah tells me January, July's sister, takes care of Heather, the baby, while July is away. "I'd love for you to meet them soon. You'll see July's not like other celebrities. She's down to earth, does only shows with inspiring stories now." I admit it would be lovely to meet them. I've heard so much about July, who championed the end of angel fever sweeping the town with media and looky-loos.

Thinking Noah's worldly mind might have some suggestions, "What do you think we should do about Emma Rose? Should we tell others now or wait till you write an article? We can't cause more problems for the town."

"Your great grandmother feels angels are calling. Somehow, the word has to get out. It could challenge folks thinking about life, death, our world!"

As we drive down the foggy roads to my house, Noah asks, "Is there somewhere we can sit and talk awhile so we don't disturb Madam Norma and Miss Marilyn? Maybe we can sit outside on your porch?"

"Sure," I tell him. "I'll show you how we say goodnight to the moon." I laugh as he looks at me with curiosity.

"Sounds wonderful. That's what Dad and Mother and I call moon bathing."

"Why I love that name! That's what we've done for years but never thought of naming it. moon bathing!"

"Yeah, it's pretty serendipitous; we both love to stare at the night sky and stars. Nothing like it here in Mystic Bay. When the night's are clear, you can see way into our galaxy, I think...way beyond light years away." We cruise down Beach Road and park in front of our house with the yellow porch light glowing its' welcome home. We tip toe into the living room greeted by gentle King in the foyer and Blue on the stairs. Without a word, I lead him to the kitchen and out the back door with King and Blue following. We lie on the porch chaises looking at the fog-ridden sky. With only the dim light from the kitchen, we can see the salty mist envelope the back yard. There are a few stars, and the moon wrapped up in grey blankets of clouds shows only dim light. King puts his head on my lap and Blue surprises us both by jumping next to Noah. Fortunately, Noah says he's not allergic. I button my jacket, and pull up the throw; it's pretty cool now.

"This is great. Wow, moon bathing, even though the moon is hiding."

I explain, "Each night we say goodnight to God, the stars, the moon, and sacred night."

"You have a special family, Maggie. Tell me about them."

"You go first. Tell me about your life, living in New York with your parents. I want to hear everything about you."

"My life's been good. Actually, I was adopted by Mom and Dad, raised in Manhattan, spent part of the summers on Fire Island where we have a little beach cottage. I'd love to take you there sometime this summer if I could. No cars allowed except city vehicles. And deer roam free. The stars there are amazing. Oh, you can see them on our New York apartment balcony too, but Fire Island is special." Noah looks from the sky to me and I take a breath in. It sounds so romantic, a cottage on an island with him. I stop myself from thinking about it, hoping he can't read minds like GG. He continues, " I went to school at Columbia, got my Masters in Creative Writing. I've worked for the Randall Publishing firm since I took a leave to be with Dad, That's it...nothing earth shattering, just lucky to have nice parents and upbringing. Please tell me about you."

"No, keep going, please. Have you published yourself?" He's not telling me something important. I can feel it.

"One published article called, *A Boy's Psychic Journey*. I wanted to challenge myself and write an autobiography, but it's taken a back seat to Dad and finishing his detective series. He's inspired me. As I wrote about my childhood and my psychic tendencies, I realized how I'd suppressed it, blowing it off. I knew I could read people, what they were like, whether to trust them or not. I don't know where my abilities came from, obviously somewhere down the line. My parents were great. Nostalgia kicked in when Mom became ill. She wanted to move here where Dad did research for his first Connor Diamond novel. She became enthralled with the Samuel Blakley novel, **My California Angel**. Till the end of her life, she thought Hannah and her Dad might actually be angels. She was convinced. She said she thought she was becoming psychic herself living here. What do you think about that?"

I laugh, "Really, I never gave it a second thought. No one did. I've known the wonderful O'Ryan family my whole life. They're like us and other folks in town. You've met Gabe, Hannah's father, the animal whisperer. But many in this town are gifted with **psychicness**, as you call it. As far as angels living in town? Well, it's a beautiful thought."

"My mother loved angels so much, she wanted it to all be real. That's why our house and yard are filled with angels. Now little Emma Rose has seen an angel. It's just wonderful, isn't it? I know I'll write a story about it someday. I can feel it coming. Remember now, enough about me, I asked about you!"

"Please keep going, tell me more about your mother."

"Mom was a lovely person, encouraging and loving. She died a year after they moved here. Dad's diagnosis seemed to escalate when she passed away, and it's been a steady progression of dementia ever since. He goes in and out, realizing she's really gone. Dad had detailed notes for the last in the series, **The Other Side of Diamonds**. I decided I had to attempt to finish it for him and for her memory. Mother would have liked that. She always told me that writing was Dad's therapy. I go on a tour Friday for a week promoting it, then home a few days, then back again on tour. The writing world will be shocked at his diagnoses and disappointed, I suppose, that I finished the last book. My agent said I did a good job copying his style, but I know it can't compare to his genius. I wish I didn't have to leave him Friday, but he has great caregivers." Noah stops talking. "Now, Maggie, please tell me about you."

"First, let me say, I'm sorry about losing your mother, and about your father's illness. It's a wonderful thing you've done, moving here to be with your father and finishing his last work."

"Maggie, are you psychic like your grandmother and great grandmother?"

I will tell him the watered down version of the truth. I hesitate a moment listening to the hum, the lullaby of the trees.. "When I was a little girl, I felt connected to nature.

I wanted to be outside all the time, even in the cold, the rain, and blustery sand-in-your-face beach days. Spending all summer days starting in the mornings gazing at morning stars and sunrise, I waited until it was time to play with Jenny. If I wasn't in school, I stayed outdoors playing with the dogs and cats and watching all that goes on in the back yard. I don't have the abilities like Gram and GG at all. GG can read minds some and they both can see the future at times. They help people with their intuitive abilities. I use my intuition as a Special Education teacher and I have a great job at Mystic Bay Elementary starting in September. Emma Rose is in my class; Jenny's nephew, Patrick too. My sensitivity to the emotions of children with intellectual disabilities is a soulful connection."

"That's awesome, a gift! There's something about your parents. They're not psychics, are they? They don't live here, I'm thinking."

My heart aches for a moment but I'm totally honest. "My mother left when I was small. Gram and GG said she was more like my grandfather who left my mother when she was a baby; she didn't have abilities. She wanted a different life, embarrassed by Gram and GG and Mystic Bay. She changed her name, had a career as an actress. Jenny Google'd her name. She's married to some wealthy producer. I don't remember her at all. I don't know who my father is. My mother never would tell GG and Gram. She stopped communicating with them years ago." As I regurgitate it all to Noah, my stomach aches. I spill it out like a rupturing volcano. I feel the anger I know I suppress. I don't even know my parents, yet who wouldn't wish for the white picket-fenced life Noah had...a loving mom and dad, a beach house on Long Island Sound with deer roaming free?

Noah sits up and reaches for my hand. "I'm sorry, Maggie. That must be hard. Your Gram and GG are extraordinary women. I can tell they love you so much." We are quiet for a while listening to the sounds of the night. I hear the rhythmic night hum around me, especially my pine.

"Tell me more about your psychic abilities?"

As the Bishop Pine sways and hums I tell him, "It's a kind of a pulse I feel around nature, an energy. Sounds weird and hard to explain, I know." Closing my eyes, waiting for his response, I realize he's still holding my hand. "I did see a special bee with golden feathered wings twice yesterday. Actually, I saw one at your house. I have to look it up on the Internet. I've never seen anything like them before."

"Really, that's so cool. We have a book on bees at the house. I'll look it up too. Feathered wings?"

I drop the subject, commenting on the hidden moon. Noah tells me a wise friend told him the moon is God's night light. I close my eyes.

"Moon bathing under God's night light? How beautiful that is."

Noah squeezes my hand, as the night becomes midnight cold. We both yawn and I realize it's time for the most wonderful date I've ever had to end. We walk back through the warm house to the front door.

"Maggie, tomorrow night, will you come to my house? I'll order Bob's Pizza and we can go swimming. Our pool is heated and I want you to meet Dad before I leave on the book tour. I want you to get to know my funny dogs and moon bathe, too. Maybe we'll see more stars and the moon will be out tomorrow night."

Of course I say yes and thank him for the lovely evening.

Noah Greenstreet has such a handsome face. His aura glows in the beams from the front porch light.

"Come here, Maggie," he says drawing me near. Our first kiss sends me soaring. He says goodnight, then kisses me again three more times and leaves. I close the door, leaning against it. It's dark in the house except for the light on the stairs.

"Noah," I say to no one but the air. Blue is waiting on the first stair. I pet King goodnight as I pick up old Blue and walk up the stairs. King looks up at us.,

"It's okay, you want to come." I pat my leg. But he turns back into GG's room. Another beautiful white feather is in the middle of the stairway;. I pick it up. Gram's been carrying feathers around. Where did she get them? I'll put it by the other one on the nightstand.

My mind goes back to Noah. I never thought I'd meet anyone like him. He gets me. Well, the little I told him. Getting into bed, I try and try to remember him, somewhere, once upon a time... a man named Noah, his kiss, a man I've met before, the man who, just like me, loves to moon bathe.

6

The Meeting And The Moon

When I arrive home from work, there is a book on the welcome mat, the last novel in Noah's father's series, **The Other Side of Diamonds**. He must have placed it there early this morning with a note.

> *Maggie, Please give this to your Gram and GG with love.*
> *See you tonight at 6:00.*
> *P.S. I remember where we met!*
> *Noah*

All I can think about is Noah. He remembers...but where, when? As the afternoon progresses, Gram's read a fourth of the book.

"Very exciting," she remarks. "I'm going to miss that Conner Diamond, even though he's not a real man. He's so smart, utterly irresistible."

We're prepared, waiting for our guests. Before she left, Sweet Mabel made her specialties, iced tea and coffee. I made chocolate chip cookies. When everyone arrives, we sit in the afternoon sun-lit dining room with its old mahogany table and eight antique chairs.. I bring in a few extra chairs when Jack and Stella arrive with their son, Guy and daughter-in law, Bette. Guy is the editor of *The Mystic Bay Town Crier* and writes local mysteries. They're Patrick's parents. He's eight years old with dark brown hair like his dad and he sits on his daddy's lap. Stella has a manila envelope in her hand. Jenny slips in too, and gives me a hug. "Surprise," she whispers as she sits down next to Guy. Reverend Carlos and Sharon come in. Even though she's the Minister's wife, being a medium somehow goes just fine in this melting pot of a town. We welcome everyone and normally shy Elena addresses us. "Thank you for coming today. You are like family to me and, as you know now, Emma Rose spoke for the first time in her life the other day in front of Maggie. She said, "Angel." Elena has tears in her eyes. "She said it again today and called me Mama."

Everyone starts talking at once congratulating Elena. She asks me to tell the story.

"Emma Rose and I were having a picnic by the brook. I saw the apparition of my late dog Jeb and I was stunned. We followed Jeb to what I thought was a dead bird on the path. My dog vanished, but the bird rose as if held and lifted up in the air and flew away. Emma Rose pointed to it and said, 'Angel.' I thought she meant the bird at first. I really thought I was dreaming or had some type of hallucination until Elena called me."

"You're not dreaming," Jack assures me, taking Patrick on his lap.

"Tell them, Guy and Bette." Guy stands up. His dark hair has an aura around it of bluish green.

"Patrick drew a picture of an angel yesterday with his crayons. The thing is, he can't draw, can hardly scribble in a coloring book!" Stella takes the picture out of the manila envelope she's holding. A golden yellow angel has been drawn with an impressionistic flare. She's holding a small brown dog. The swirling colors are touched with pinks and blues and a halo glows around the angel like it's made of pure light. It looks like it could hang in a museum. As it is passed around the room, I can feel the silence. Then Bette and Stella begin to cry. We're awestruck. Patrick, on his Grandfather's lap, closes his eyes as a nap comes round; unaware of the incredible art he's created.

Reverend Carlos stands, "This is God's miracle. We need to tell the world. The angels are telling us they are here through these beautiful children! Perhaps they are showing themselves because of the town's good works, the animals' lives we are saving, the children being fostered, adopted."

GG stays seated but says in almost a whisper, "As the oldest psychic in town, I must tell you; since we all started to do a little more for this world, I have felt something like this was coming, something with the angels. We must be very careful what we do now. We can't expose the children to any exploitation from the outside. Remember Hannah and Gabe's experience with the media when that book came out? We must inform them, yet tread carefully. I think we should wait and proceed with absolute caution. I feel more is coming, more angels will show themselves."

Elena blurts out, "I made a big mistake and told Emma Rose's father, Jamie. I couldn't help it. He never comes around, but came over yesterday for the first time in a long time to ask to borrow money. He heard Emma Rose say "Angel." Like a fool I told him what happened. Now he wants to go to the media, like news stations and STARZ Magazine to get paid for the story. I shouldn't have told him.. I feel so bad; I'm scared now."

"It's okay, Elena," Jack assures her. Perhaps you can ward him off. Tell him a friend of yours will give him some money to help him out. I'll do it, bide some time till we know how to handle him. Does everyone agree?"

"Wait," GG says calmly, her sharp mind racing through the problem. "I have an idea. You just send him over to see Marilyn, Maggie and me tomorrow afternoon. Tell him we're going to talk to him about how he will get money and soon, a little bank account. Jack, a little money is a good idea. We'll fix him up just fine. He won't talk after we see him, if everything goes according to plan."

Everyone looks at her with astonishment, not knowing what she means. But I do. Oh wow, my great-grandmother is going to blow their minds with her plans to stop deadbeat dad, Jamie Bond, in his tracks. His name really is Jamie Bond. 007 he's not. The psychic plans of one shrewd old lady at 20 Moon Road start a-brewing in that lovely curly white-haired one hundred year plus old head.

～～

Noah and I enter the warm dark water. It barely ripples. The moon peeks out from the clouded sky. His dogs lie on the stone deck watching us with interest. Noah brought me in the house to meet his ailing father. "Hello, young lady," is all he said, but it was enough for me to see the kindness and contentment in his eyes. His caregivers, Lorraine and Cal, took him to the kitchen where they'd prepared a roast to his liking. Noah and I swim in the heated pool and I explain the events of the day, how little Patrick Benfield has colored a miracle, an amazing angel. Learning of his intellectual disability, Noah is utterly astonished. When he hears of GG's plan for Elena's husband, he laughs heartily.

"Your great-grandma is a wonder. More messages from heaven? This is clearly happening in our time. You realize, Maggie, it started the day we met again." We get out, wrapping towels around us.

Noah is being coy about where we met; teasing me that he's not going to tell me. We're having fun playing with his friendly dogs. We have a glass of wine and veggie pizza before we swim again and talk like we've known each other for years.

"Noah, please tell me where we met or can I guess?"

But all he says slyly is, " You have to remember yourself in order for it to be extraordinary that we found each other again."

Then his face turns serious as he looks at me. Where, when was it our lives crossed? It must be as children, I'm guessing. Or was in New York City when I visited as a teenager with Jenny and her family. Or was it LA or college? "Okay," I finally acquiesce. "I'll ask my psychic side to remember but I don't want to have sleepless nights. My mind races at night now these last few days."

"You'll remember, Maggie Joy, and when you do, you'll fly to my doorstep. I can see it in my mind's eye." Embarrassed again, I go to Noah's room to change. His mother decorated the room with orange and yellow prints, to accent the room's teak furniture. With its mid-century style, it renders an alluring hominess. I can always feel love inside a true home and this one has it. I wish I'd met his mother, Josephine. I see a photo of her on the dresser. A beauty she was, a professional model when his dad met her; she had long dark hair and gorgeous deep-set eyes. By her photo is a collection of tiny angels.

Dressed and outside again by the pool, we comment on the beauty of the night. The moon finally peeks hello amid the fog. As I gaze at the moon, trying to forget he won't be home for a week, the dogs start running around the pool in chase. Noah says to them, "Swim time!" Shadow jumps in, but Smarty, Murph and Nursie don't. Shadow has waited his turn and swims, frolicking with delight. Smarty decides to get into his play pool.

Noah remarks, "Gabe is such an amazing dog psychic. He said Smarty's afraid of the large pool because he was thrown in as a puppy but he wants to join in so I bought him his own kiddy pool. Nursie watches Shadow like a hawk and Murphy always stands glued to her. The little ones don't like the water." Shadow is pretty comical, almost swimming in laps; we dry the dogs when they get out. They do their doggy shake, drenching us again. When they're pretty dry, we go back into the house. Lorraine and Cal are getting Noah's dad ready for bed and we're alone in the living room with the dogs beside us. We sit for a while gazing at the river rock gas lit fireplace. Another night I don't want to end.

"This is nice, Noah. I love your beautiful house, your dogs and your dad is so sweet. Lorraine and Cal are marvelous with him."

Noah agrees. "Thanks, I've tried my best to keep him comfortable. It's sad to see his once brilliant mind leave. I wish you could have known him before his illness. He didn't have the ego that some very successful people have. He always kept a low profile, loving to write his novels at home, especially at our cottage on Fire Island. All I can do is be with him now as he fades."

"I know you must be a great comfort to him. Please tell me about his first book and Mystic Bay."

"He once said he interviewed psychics in towns up and down the coast but he heard about Mystic Bay's psychics and how they stood out, all genuine, not a fake among them. My mother said he thought the town was enchanted though he never told me that. Mystic Bay may be enchanted, Maggie. Did you ever think of that?"

I have to laugh, "It is rather an enchanting place. When I lived in LA, I think I forgot how very beautiful it is or how the folks are so different."

"You never read the first novel, **One Psychic Summer**, did you?"

I marvel at his psychicness and have to admit I never have read any of the series but would like to. Noah says he'll send me home with his father's first. He says I'll surely pick GG and Gram out, although it was meant all to be kept anonymous.

"I didn't know they were in the book as characters."

"Yes," Noah replies. "He disguised the psychics here, yet wrote them as real characters. My dad changed their names, of course. He loved picking out the names and writing the characters' unique personalities. He said the characters became real people to him, like friends who never disappoint you. He loved the town and told me he wished he'd never left, that he and mom had raised me here instead of New York."

"It will be fun to figure out who's who! My Gram and GG are real characters for sure in real life. The whole town's full of them."

The night finally comes to an end. Noah takes me home. Walking me to my door, he puts his arms around me. As we stand and kiss in the cool late night, I feel the heavy fog swirl around us as if it's bringing us closer still. I don't want him to leave. He must go on to his book signings and I must tend to the tasks at hand, with GG's cleverness to thwart Jamie

Bond's motives and keep the children's identity a secret if possible.

From the front window, I watch his car move down Moon Road then turn on Beach Road, disappearing in the fog up Bluff Road to his house. I realize I was so swept up in the night, I forgot to take the book home. Wherever did I meet the man before? He said I would remember. His kind nature is almost too good to be true. He doesn't find me freakish like so many others would. No, Noah Connor Greenstreet seems almost heaven sent.

7

The Wiley Ways Of Psychic Ladies

GG took the idea from a plot in one of the Connor Diamond Series best books, **Connor Diamond and the Magic Crystal Ball.**

Gram has summoned Mr. Jamie Bond to the parlor for tea to discuss the angel, little Emma Rose, tabloids, and money. Since Elena told us how superstitious he was we dressed in gypsy attire complete with colored scarves and lots of bright shiny beads. There is a candle burning on the table and a little crystal ball lava lamp plugged into the wall next to it. I sit on the sidelines with Blue on my lap, a red scarf like mine tied around his head. Jamie sits in the darkened parlor downing the hot tea he wants mixed with six lumps of sugar, all the while staring at big but harmless King sitting next to me. King is wearing a scarf with dogs and cats on it. On the man, a little brow of sweat is forming and his shirt is wet under the arms.

"That dog doesn't bite, does he?"

"Not usually," Gram says sighing. "However, he did bite the mailman once." Jamie shifts nervously in his chair, waiting but never taking his eyes off King. There is a long silence.

He looks at me, "Your cat is cross-eyed, you know."

"He's in a trance," I say softly.

Gram begins, "Are you aware, Mr. James Bond, that we are the wisest psychic ladies in town. Did you know we speak to spirits?"

"Yeah," says Jamie shifting. " Elena told me. Call me Jamie; I get teased about my damn name all the time. And listen, I'm from Riverton, so I don't know many people here since Elena moved out to that house on Meadowbrook. But she told me about you psychics. She said your daughter here babysits my kid for free. Thanks. What's your name?"

"Maggie," I respond politely even though I already introduced myself at the door.

"Maggie, you're all kinda weird. Do you dress like this all the time?"

Not getting a response he points to old Cookie lying on the floor sleeping peacefully with scarf on her head and her latest cartoon diaper peeking past the dress. "That dog looks dead."

"No, in a trance, just like the cat. Did you know that people fear my grandmother and great grandmother's powers," I whisper loudly to him.

Gram lies the lie she must, "We are in touch with spirits, sir, and they are in touch with the angels in town. They talk to us each day. My mother, Madam Norma here is one of the most famous psychics in California. She will speak into this crystal ball and summon them."

GG uses a gravelly voice, "Oh spirits and protective angels, are you here? Please tell us what to do about Mr. Bond here wanting to make money from his daughter's vision."

She looks down deep into the oily crystal ball rubbing her hands around it. She moans, "Ummmm." Then she pretends to listen to someone talking to her by placing her head next to the ball.

"Ah, they have spoken. The spirits say the angels are telling us you must remain quiet about this now. If you do, money will line your pockets. They say the child needs to be protected. You must promise never to say her name or show her photo to anyone in the media. She is a gift to us all, and the angel came to her to send a message to the world. Do you promise, Mr. Bond?"

"I thought you guys were gonna get me money; that's what Elena said. She said you talk to angels. Hell, I need it bad," says Jamie clearly upset now. "I want money for me and," he hesitates… " And, uh, for Emma Rose, too." We glance at each other, knowing he's only thinking of himself.

Just like the plot in the book, GG hands him the big fakeout. "Yes, what? Oh yes, the spirits say there's an eight-foot angel standing behind you." Jamie jumps turning around in his chair.

GG continues, "The angel insists you must be quiet now or he will send King here to be with you night and day to make sure you don't say a thing. He will fly King there on angel's wings. Right, King?"

King jumps and barks. Jamie looks like he might soil himself, leaping up and running behind Gram's chair.

"Oh, he won't hurt you," Gram tries gently to fake soothe his mind putting her hand on his. "Remember, now the angels want it a secret. Then I promise you, you will be the richest man in all of Riverton." She leads Jamie back to his chair. He looks at King with wide-eyed fear. King stares him down and licks his lips. What Jamie doesn't know is that we have a dog treat under the table waiting for him when we are finished. GG's got him trained big time.

"I don't know. Why would they make me wait?" Jamie Bond isn't stupid but he is naïve. Elena says his superstitious mind makes him turn the car around if a black cat runs in front of it. He throws salt over his left shoulder when he spills it and thinks Mystic Bay is a psycho place where only witches and mentally ill people live. He believes it all. He's really afraid of gentle, wouldn't-hurt-a-fly, King. Well, maybe a fly.

GG encourages Jamie to sit down in front of the table again as she takes his hand, "Look into my eyes, Mr. Bond." Jamie does as told and GG starts to hypnotize the unsuspecting Jamie. "You are tired, your eyes grow weary but you are listening to me so deep in your soul. Listen, listen! My voice is strong and you will do what I say now and not speak to anyone about Emma Rose and the angels. You will protect your little daughter for many years. You will be a better man and look for work. You will feel rich with blessings." She speaks in a almost a whisper, "Now, wake up refreshed, remembering everything the spirits and angels have told us."

Jamie wakes up and GG continues in a soft voice as if she didn't hypnotize him.

"The angels know you are a good man. You will have a bank account opened at Pacific Trust Bank for you and Emma Rose tomorrow with two hundred dollars in it. You can use one hundred of it now, but must leave the rest there and wait. More money will come every two weeks till things are better for you financially. It will be wonderful." GG is smiling, delighted with her act.

"Just don't let that dog come live with me? Promise?" I can tell he's afraid to turn around in his chair. "Is the angel gone? Make him promise. I'll be quiet then. But I need more money than just one hundred dollars while I look for work."

"Oh, you will, dear Mr. Bond. Right, King?"

King jumps and barks again and Jamie's eyes almost pop out of his head.

"You ladies and that dog scare me. Please tell the angel to leave and get the dog out of here so I can go now."

"Of course, Mr. Bond. Why, that angel just flew away and now King, 'Le supper'! She claps her hands.

King gets up and trots into the kitchen, knowing that's his signal to wait for his dinner.

Jamie stands up. "Well, goodbye I guess. You psychics are sure different." With newfound confidence since King is gone, he stretches. "Can't wait for my money for sure. You ladies promise, right?"

"Oh yes, dear Jamie," says Gram. "Why, I think you'll be getting a new car, too.. Stay in your apartment at night unless you're looking for work. The angels will be watching. They'll tell us if you've kept your part of the bargain. Or else King will surely have to be flown by that eight-foot angel to live with you and we would miss him, wouldn't we, dears?"

GG and I say, "Yes," in unison.

" Oh dear, that won't be fun for you, Jamie Bond." Gram smiles a half smile.

"What? Oh God, okay. Goodbye. Thanks, I guess." Jamie almost runs out of the house to his waiting beat-up truck. Gram goes to the front door and waves.

"Goodbye, Mr. Bond. Stay safe and mums the word!"

She puts her long fake black nail-polished finger to her lips. Jamie drives away like a racecar driver driving a lemon...exhaust pluming.

Sitting down, I can't help it. I start crying and laughing at the same time. GG gets up, holding on to Gram. They do a standing waltz. Gram laughs, "The old fake crystal ball trick always works for people with bad intentions. Sorry to put angels in the mix today, but I think they understand our motives."

GG says, "The power of suggestion will help for awhile, I hope. It's the best I can do." King comes back out wondering where his dinner is. GG taught him "le supper" means dinnertime, but he already ate. "King, you deserve a treat!" King almost smiles. She reaches under the table for the dog biscuit. Blue tries like heck to take the scarf off, his head rolling around the carpet. I take it off laughing. "Good trance moves, Blue." Cookie still lies on the carpet with her apparent dead dog trick. Gram speaks in a loud voice, as Cookie is pretty deaf, "Treat time." Cookie slowly gets up and stretches.

I look at my dancing great grandmother and grandmother standing, arms in motion like they're on *Dancing With The Stars*. "You two, that was total genius! But you know we can't really trust that guy. Now what?"

"Mr. James Bond just might surprise all of us," GG says with a glint in her psychic eyes.

8

Past Meets Present

The wind is blowing. Emma Rose and I are picnicking again by the stream. The trees sway their rhythmic hum, soothing my soul. I can see their reflections in the rippling water. This week Elena was thrilled as Emma Rose said "Angel" and "Mama" again. Looking toward the direction she's pointing, my heart dances. Jeb is there once more. His golden coat flies up with the breeze. His eyes sparkle at me and I feel joy rather than heartache. Getting up slowly, taking Emma Rose's hand, the little girl lets go and starts to run. "Angel chase butterfly." She runs after a yellow butterfly giggling with delight. After a few seconds she stops. I look for Jeb, but he is gone. The angel appeared to her again and she said three words! The angel beckoned her to chase the butterfly with her...how lovely, how extraordinary! Why am I present to see this miraculous sight? What do I have to do with angels calling?

It's been a long night at the restaurant and it's only ten. I've talked to Noah every day this week. We've talked very little about his book tour, mostly about Emma Rose and Patrick's sightings of the angels. Gram and GG are thrilled I'm seeing Jeb. "It's another blessing from the angels," says GG. Noah has a friend whose dad is an entomologist. He's calling me tomorrow about the bee I spotted. He wants a photo of it if possible, but I haven't seen it since the day I met Noah. Jenny and I were going shopping for my maid of honor dress tomorrow, but Jack and Stella have called us all to meet again at two. This time the meeting is at Hannah's house behind their store off Main Street. We're meeting to discuss what to do before the media gets wind of the sightings, since Emma Rose has had her second encounter and Patrick has painted a watercolor. Guy, Bette, Stella, and Jack emailed us all that the angel is a wonder to see... more beautiful than the first one. Noah tells me his psychic vibe says Jamie Bond will keep quiet. He thinks he's an odd kind of guy, almost comical, and he'd make a great character in a novel. That's pretty funny. Still it's hard to believe he'll really keep his mouth closed, but we will see.

Noah's picking me up at work before eleven if his plane gets in on time and I can hardly stand the waiting. There is a couple at the bar and a few customers in the restaurant including Doc Nathan and his wife Terry. They're paying their check when I see a guy walk in the restaurant. What? It's Brian, my ex! What's he doing here? I feel the rush of nerves run to the pit of my stomach. He looks the same, brown hair, mustache, and blue green cat-like eyes; still as good-looking as ever. My ex orders a beer and Tad pours him a draft. The claws-out Missy, wearing black leather jeans and a tight halter-top, starts talking to him.

"What on earth are you doing here?" My voice is raised, walking up to him, interrupting her. "I'm working."

"Hey, Maggie. Your Grandma said you were here when I called your house. Why'd you change your cell number and email? I've been trying to call you for at least a month. I need to talk to you."

"I've nothing to say. So leave." I turn to go, but he holds my arm.

"Maggie, please. I'll wait till you're ready to go home. I've something important to tell you, please." He looks dejected. Heidi must have broken up with him. He so hates to be alone. I try to pull away, but he keeps hold of me.

Tad pipes up, "Hey, you heard the lady. She's wants you to leave. Anyway, she's got a new boyfriend." I look at Tad who's smirking while Missy's mouth parts in surprise.

"Oh yeah, that was fast," Brian says, obviously upset, letting go of me now. "What's his name?" I can't speak, but

Tad's happy to announce, "He's that good looking guy who comes in for take out a lot, Noah Greenstreet."

"Noah Greenstreet from New York?" Missy seems utterly amazed. "The player of the western world? You better run, Girl. He dumped my friend Gwen. He's even worse than Mr. Tad Jones here."

"I heard that," remarks Tad with a laugh as he pours her another glass of Merlot.

Missy looks me up and down. "You're not his type at all. I doubt he's ever dated a server. He likes tall, pretty blonds, sophisticated like me, although I never met the jerk." She laughs, taunting me, taking a sip of her wine.

Brian is incensed and yells loudly, "Maggie is a thousand times prettier than you!"

"Hold it down now," says Tad, "or Jack will come out here. You're both fine looking women, okay?" Missy gives Tad a look that would kill and storms off her chair to another one at the end of the bar.

Brian looks at me with that little lost boy face that always drew me in. "Look, Maggie. Yes, I'd like to be back in your life. I realize I'm a major screw-up for breaking up and dating Heidi, but that was short-lived." He whispers in my ear, "I found out your mother, Lyla Jasmine, might just lead me to your real father. I have some big leads."

―– ―

When I get my head out of a fog, I realize I fainted. Now I'm lying on the couch in Jack's office with Brian and Doc

Nathan standing over me. Jenny is kneeling down holding my hand while Jack is pacing back and forth.

"Maggie, are you okay?" Brian sounds sincere. "I'm sorry. I didn't mean to upset you."

Doc Nathan, our next-door neighbor says, "She's okay. But here, Maggie dear, drink some water." Doc Nathan helps me take a sip from the glass. "She'll be all right," he remarks. "Maggie, rest awhile and drink water and go home to bed, okay? No more work tonight. Jenny, can you take her home?" Jenny says, "Of course."

"Maggie, call me if you need anything and I'll come over." He starts to leave, but there's a knock at the office door. It's Noah, upset and clearly worried. He was going to pick me up and now our night is ruined. We were going to sit under the stars and moon bathe. His face says it all. He's wondering who Doc Nathan and Brian are.

"They told me you fainted, that some guy upset you. Are you all right?"

"I'm fine."

"Who are you?" Noah looks Brian over.

"I'm her boyfriend, Brian Morris. And you?" Brian is mad.

"You've got it wrong, dude, I'm her boyfriend, actually." Boyfriend? We only had two dates and talked on the phone everyday for a week. I try to get up but feel weak and sit down again. Jack and Doc Nathan talk low to both men.

"She needs rest now," says Doc, looking at Noah.

"Can you take her home now?" Noah says.

"Yes, sure. Is she all right?" He helps me up. Doc Nathan continues. "She'll be fine, but call me with any problems." He gives Noah his card. "I live right next door to Maggie."

Brian gets up almost trembling. He gives Noah a dirty look, and then shifts to me. "Call me when you wake up. I'm staying at the Riverton Inn Motel. I need to talk to you before I head back to LA tomorrow. You know my cell. Take care, Maggie."

He looks at me with such a hurt expression that I almost feel sorry for him. He looks at Noah. "And don't call me dude." He leaves and everyone looks at each other. Jenny starts to laugh. "Chalk one up for you, Noah." There's some chuckling between the men which is funny since I've just fainted, but I go along with it. "Sorry...it's like a bad reality TV show."

Noah helps me up with his arm around me. Jack walks out to the door with us. "You don't have to come to work tomorrow, Maggie."

"I'm fine Jack. I'll be there just as always. It was just a shock seeing him is all."

Brian says he knows who my mother is; I never told him her stage name. He's somehow found out clues about my real father. Tears form in my eyes. Why? I don't care about my parents. As we walk to the restaurant door, Tad and Missy walk up. "You okay, Maggie," asks Tad.

"Yes, I'm fine really. Tad, you know Noah." I don't introduce Missy. I just ignore her like she's a fly on the wall, but of course, she has to get her two cents in.

" Hey Noah, I'm Missy, Gwen Anderson's friend from New York. I told your poor little Maggie here, I heard you were a real player then, a real jerk to Gwen."

"Missy, come on." Tad is furious, I can tell. She tweaks my anger, but I relax and have to laugh out loud when Noah retorts, "Player? You've got it wrong. I was immature once, that's true. Now, I've found myself lucky to be mature enough to find a lovely, quality woman. You should try a healthy relationship sometime." Missy is silent as we finally leave, but Tad calls to me, "Take care, Maggie." Missy gives him a swat with her purse.

I close my eyes as Noah drives in silence the block and a half to my house. We walk in and find King waiting; Gram and GG are obviously asleep. King walks up the stairs to my bedroom with us. We find the cat in his usual spot on the bed. King settles down and Noah pets Blue. "I'll be right back," I say to the sweetest man ever as I go into the bathroom.

When I come out, he's standing looking at me. I must be a real vision wearing my black sheep pajamas. They're my favorite, white with black sheep all over them with red bows around their necks. They're so soft and I'm so tired; I just had to put them on.

"Come here, Maggie, cute pj's. Let's talk about this. I'm staying till you fall asleep. Can I tuck you in?" My heart pitter pats, seeing him in my bedroom. He smiles and I almost faint again. I get in bed and Noah puts the covers around me. Blue snuggles at my feet and Noah sits next to me. King stays on the floor wagging his tail. He's never done that. He always stays with GG.

"All those years I was with Brian, I never told him my mother was Lyla Jasmine. I just told him I didn't know who my father was. He's a law clerk now and for some reason decided to find out about my parents. Now he says he has leads on my father. I'm trying to process it all. Brian was never interested in my life. Why start now? I don't want to know who my father is anymore. My father didn't know about me or didn't care." I close my eyes; Noah puts his arms around me.

"It's okay, Maggie. It'll be all right," he whispers. My eyes can't stay open any longer. He asks me a question, but I can't speak. He stays awhile as I go in and out of sleep. He turns the light off. I feel a kiss on my forehead. *Don't go*, I want to shout but can't.

9

The Man I Used To Love

The sun's first pale light brightens the horizon as I meet Noah on the road with our dogs. The month of July is spectacular with blue-sky mornings streaked with peach, grey and purple hues. A morning star winks from light years away. The moon hangs two hundred fifty thousand or so miles away, serene and storybook white. We breathe in the salty air watching the dogs sniffing each other. King finds happiness with his new pack of jogging partners. The paintbrush pastel colors disappear as quickly as they came. We slowly jog towards the tiny harbor, the sun rising over the hills. Noah said he was surprised to see me up and ready to jog with him, but I wanted to tell him how

I appreciated his care, how I'm fine. Am I fine? I know I'm adrenaline pumped up from last night.

" I don't want anyone hurting you ever," he says sincerely.

We slow jog and King keeps in step with the others. On the way Noah stops to pick up Murphy and Nursie as the little shaggy black and white dogs get tired. He somehow manages two leases and two dogs in his arms. We say our long goodbyes at the entrance to the alley. Knowing I will see him tonight feels like a dream. Noah tells me not to worry, that all will be well. He feels it in his soul. "I'm here, and we'll figure this all out. Do you want me to be with you when you meet Brian? Just say the word."

This wonderful man has come into my life, but it's all so unreal. Now I must face Brian.

"Thanks, Noah. I need to handle him myself. I'll be fine. I plan on telling him never to contact me again."

"Okay, just call my cell if you need me, promise?" He kisses me and jogs away with his flock of dogs. I turn to go up the alley but see Mr. Beasley approaching, hearing first his whistle, his hello.

"Mornin', Mr. Beasley."

"Morning, dear Maggie and King, my boy." He stops as usual to pet King and we talk about the beautiful sunrise. Seagulls play tag and dive for fish around us, then fly up high in unison to move on to wherever their next catch is. "Have a good day," he calls as he walks on and begins his tune again.

Calling Brian's cell as I'm about to walk into work, he surprises me by asking if I'm okay? This makes my blood boil; yet I agree to meet at *The Next Door Café* at twelve. What does he know about Polly Ann, about me, about my father?

~ ~

By twelve thirty, Brian and I are in the packed restaurant, have each ordered iced tea, and Brian has ordered the special, the giant BLT Stevie bragged about. I've insisted I'm not hungry. My stomach churns. I wave to a few people I know. Brian says too loudly, "Look at the guy by the window. He's eating his sandwich like a squirrel eats nuts!" I turn around to see Andy Walin eating the giant BLT turning it round and round reminiscent of Bubbles, Hannah's dad's pet squirrel.

I turn back to Brian remarking, "Andy sure is one clever sandwich eater."

"Weird dude. Just like the rest of your psycho town." Before I can get a jab in Laurjean swishes by with her hair swept up in her usual colored pen to match her clothes. Today she wears canary yellow pants and shirt and a yellow pen to hold her silvery bun up. Yellow sneakers don her feet.

"New in town, are we?" She asks him but doesn't wait for an answer. She slips on by with her iced tea pitcher. She obviously doesn't remember him as he made landfall in Mystic Bay only a few times over the years, though I brought him here once. Brian wears jeans and a grey shirt and his hair looks like he didn't try to comb it. I wear my hair in a slicked back ponytail because I know he hates it that way. In fact, I wear my bright orange shirt and jacket. knowing he said once it made me look matronly.

Looking at him as he apologizes again, I can't believe I wasted over three years with him. Yet I learned so much about love, about myself, didn't I?

"You look good, Maggie, even though I like your hair down. I know I've blown it, now that you have that rich dude, Noah what's his name?"

He's being sarcastic. I don't respond.

" Maybe you'll want to hook up again though after you hear me out."

I say nothing.

Laurjean brings out his sandwich pronto. It's like she knew he was going to order it. Brian takes a big bite out of his BLT. I remember how I always thought he loved food more than me. He wipes his mouth on the napkin and looks at me with a hint of elation. He handles the manila envelope he brought.

"Okay, now I've got to tell you about your mother, Lyla Jasmine, aka Polly Ann Malone. All the info I've got is in this envelope. She went to UCLA, right, the years eighty-two and three? I had her tailed for weeks by this PI I know. He logged her cell records. It's against the law, but I did it for you. She's obsessed with her fourth husband, Sid Wasserman, and some other men. It's pretty pathetic...three of the guys went to UCLA the same years she did. But the big news is she had a call from your boss, Jack Benfield, and met him for lunch last week in Riverton at the Paradisio Hotel Patio. Their heads were together whispering. He left in a huff after he slapped money for the check on the table. Here's their photo."

Brian takes his phone out and shows me the unbelievable truth. Jack and my mother are sitting in a booth with heads bent forward talking. She looks stunning with her long blonde streaked hair, beautiful face, and a white blouse and jeans. Jack looks angry. My feet feel glued to the tile floor.

My mouth opens, but I can't speak. The ice in my tea is melting and I'm melting in my chair. Brian has actually found out about the men in her life. One is Jack Benfield, Jenny's dad, close friend of our family. That's impossible! Jack and Stella are happy, been together for years. Jenny and I are a month apart in age. No one ever said anything about there being a connection. Gram would know about this, surely. My concentration leaves me. My hands go to my face, covering my mouth.

"Maggie, say something." Brian downs his sandwich but keeps his eyes on me. With a mouth too full of sandwich, he continues, "Jack Benfield looks like you a little; you know, that dark hair and all. Hey, Jenny's mom is a blond, right? Hey, she could be your real sister! It's a chance he's your dad since why would he have a tête-à-tête with her like that? And the other guys? I think she has affairs with old boyfriends; it's all in the file I made for you." He looks smug, still eating. "Jack didn't hug your mother at the restaurant. He looked pissed the whole time, the PI said. And your real birth records only say father unknown. That's weird, Maggie. We never talked about this stuff; you kept it to yourself."

Brian looks ugly to me now. How could I ever have been attracted to a man that would just blurt out such sensitive information without even asking my permission? I have to think about this. My heart is racing, and I'm incredibly light-headed again.

Amazingly, Mr. Beasley is by my side, his hand on my shoulder. "Everything okay, Maggie?" I look up at his face, his tall stature, his white mustache and red-orange glasses, and almost shout. "My old boyfriend here is messing in my life. I want him to stop!"

Getting up abruptly, Brian announces, "Forget it. I'm leaving. Really you don't get it, do you, Maggie? I did this for you!"

He ignores Mr. B, slaps a twenty on the table mirroring Jack Benfield in his report and goes, leaving the envelope in front of me.

Mr. Beasley leans down and says, "It'll be okay, Maggie. I'm sorry if I scared him away."

"No, thank you for coming over. I didn't see you." He smiles and we say goodbye and I sit there alone.

Laurjean comes over. " Honey, bring that Noah back here and lose that other guy okay? I brought his old sandwich out fast so he'd speed up and go. Jerk old boyfriends need to amscray. You know what that means?" I shake my head no. "It means scram." She hugs me and I leave with a quiet thank you.

Laurjean must have remembered him but acted like she didn't. She just might be psychic herself. As I walk out the door to head for Hannah's and the meeting, it begins to rain. Clouds burst, the light rain swirls with the wind. I didn't even notice the change in the weather. I curl up my jacket collar. My stomach churns knots as I run across Main Street towards Hannah's store, the manila envelope tightly carried under my jacket.

10

The Wind, The Awakening

"Hey Taylor," I say to Hannah's great friend and business partner composing myself. "How are you?" I shut the door as tightly as I can with the wind and notice how Jesse, the store's resident cat, stares at me from her perch in the family's pink and green store window of Dear Dogs, Etc.

Taylor Msumba is a tall good-looking man from Batswana with skin rich like coffee and eyes that seem to sparkle even more than ever today. "Maggie Joy, it's a real joy to see you back home to stay. Welcome back." He gives me a quick hug and a little laugh. "Did you hear that Hattie and I are adopting another little girl? We are going to name her Joy. What do you think of that?"

"Taylor, that's terrific news. I would love that. I do love the name, of course. Congratulations!"

"Thank you so much." A customer walks in and so he says, " I think they're all over there now for the meeting. Helen's promised me cinnamon rolls for keeping the shop going, so make sure she saves one."

He smiles and then I hear it...a rustle like wings of a large bird. I look around... nothing. I look at him and he smiles. His eyes shine like deep brown stars mixed with golden light; his face has a glow to it I've never noticed. There's a pale pink aura around him now. I shake my head. What's wrong with me? I mutter a "thanks" and "see you later with that cinnamon roll," and head for the back door, out to the alley where everyone parks their cars, and across the yard to Hannah's house.

I take my shoes off at the back door. The smell of cinnamon rolls wafts in the air as I walk in. Hannah's endearing Aunt Helen and the lovely Sharon Manual are playing with the kids at the kitchen table. There's Emma Rose, Patrick and the ginger twins, Kate and Gabe, who sit in high chairs. The pink retro kitchen is a favorite of mine, mid-century, so classic. The family dogs and their pet deer, Dawn, lie on dog beds and a white cat sits on top of the fridge. I hug the ladies, then stoop down and hug Emma Rose, who's eating her roll. She says nothing. But as I hug Patrick, he announces with a mouth full, "Maggie, sing."

Helen says, "My, isn't that grand? He wants you to sing." Sharon nods. "These children are our miracles now. They're both talking!"

"Oh, Maggie," Helen announces, picking up a plate of rolls, "Jenny's asked me to make your maid of honor dress if that's okay with you. I can't wait to shop for fabric. You know I love pink so much, and to sew for you would be a treat."

"Thank you. How nice of you," I say back...back to present, thinking of the wedding and not all my problems.

"Maggie, sing," Patrick repeats, standing this time, his hands trying to wrap around my waist. "I will later, okay?" I ruffle his hair. As I go into the living room, I say to Helen, "Don't forget Taylor's cinnamon roll; he's dreaming of it." She smiles and winks, "I made him a dozen." She starts humming. Maybe I'll fix her up with Mr. Beasley. What a duet that would be.

The room is full of conversation as I greet everyone. Stella and Jack sit on the couch with Bette talking to Guy who sits on the floor. Hannah and Josh are standing talking to July North and a woman who looks like her twin. She must be January, her sister. July sits in a wingback holding her baby daughter, Heather Angel. Since Hannah's book came out, there have been many little girls born in the last two years whose names have included Angel. Taylor and Hattie's one-year-old daughter's name is Michelle Angel. Mayor Willie Walin sits in a wingback also and Hannah's dad Gabe sits on another chair. He plays Santa every year at the different charity events for kids in the nearby towns and looks like he really could be Kris Cringle. He dresses up Dawn, the fawn, as Rudolph. Of course, this lively older man has his funny pet squirrel, Bubbles, perched on his shoulder. She chatters loudly, eyeing the rolls. He gives her a crumb and she almost grins. Bubbles decides to go rogue and sees a piece of cinnamon roll drop to the floor from Willie's fingers. She grabs it and runs under Gabe's chair and twirls it round and round. It makes me laugh cause' it reminds me of Andy at the café. Helen is offering iced tea and coffee placed on the dining room table. Out of the blue, I hear the sound again, rustles of wings. Looking around the room for a bird or the source of the noise, I see nothing. The sound stops abruptly as it came.

When I meet July North, I'm amazed at her composure, her friendly manner. She doesn't seem like a celebrity at all. Her brunette hair shines and she wears a bright orange sweater just the color of my jacket. Her eyes have an amazing starry sparkle. And she has an aura too. Hers is reddish purple, so beautiful. January looks like July, especially her deep brown eyes that sparkle like her sister's. Her aura is blue like her sweater. What on earth is happening to me?

Mayor Willie begins as everyone settles down with coffee or drinks in hand. "We've called this second meeting with some new faces, Hannah, Gabe, Josh, January and July who we've brought up to date. Thank you for sharing your home with us, Gabe, Hannah and Josh. We welcome you, January and July. We are the planning committee now. What are we planning, you ask? Well, July and I have ideas. We know we must have an action plan for these incredible angel sightings. Elena can't be here today because of work, but we will keep her abreast of what we decide. Madam Norma and Miss Marilyn send their regrets, but Maggie and Jack will tell us the progress with Elena's ex–husband, Jamie Bond. Now, let's get started. Maggie, tell us how it went with Jamie and Madam Norma's ingenious intervention."

I sigh, composing myself, knowing many psychic abilities fill the room. Gabe and Willie are intuitive and the others are used to it. I wonder about January and July but know they are keenly aware of the town's reputation.

"Well, my great-grandmother and grandmother were amazing, really. The séance and power of suggestion seemed to work for the moment. Jamie agreed not to say anything to the press but does want to have the money put into his new bank account every two weeks as GG suggested until he finds work and is stable financially. We just don't know how long the hypnosis will work. He left pretty scared since GG told him an eight foot angel would fly my dog King to come live with him if he said anything to the press." Everyone laughs.

"That part was right out of a comedy skit. But we really don't know if it worked; the power of suggestion could tank or stay."

Everyone thinks Gram and GG are remarkable and a discussion starts about it. Jack interjects about the bank account he's in charge of, but my mind wanders. I look over at him, this teddy bear of a kind man, wondering why he would meet with my mother, what possible reason would he have? Could he be my biological father? His hair and skin sort of match my own, but I don't see any resemblance. I must be staring at him because he looks and smiles at me.

Jack agrees, "Yes, everyone. Apparently, Jamie Bond is a little shaken over this, like a martini. Please tell Madam Norma and Marilyn how we all appreciate the theatrics. And he is taking the money out though Elena says she hasn't seen or heard from him since he left Madam Norma's Parlor. He's the fly in the ointment. It may be nothing to worry about. I mean, he may not seem credible to anyone in the press. But we do need a plan and soon."

"Tell them now," Stella whispers putting her hand on his. I get goose bumps.

Jack takes a painting out of the folder. "Patrick picked up Bette's paints and this is what he painted yesterday." Three angels of different ethnicities, two female and one male grace the pastel canvas. They are singing, mouths forming an O. They are wearing robes of luminous white. The background is of the stars, indigo night, and a crescent moon. It reminds me of Van Gough's "*The Starry Night.*"

"Maggie, Patrick says the angels told him you must sing for the world." His eyes fill with tears, as do many in the room. I feel stuck to my card table chair. My olive skin should be turning white as snow. Looking again at the magical painting, I think about Patrick painting it with his mother's paints, on the floor of his house, how he looked up at me, hands clasped around me and told me to sing.

"Yes, of course but w-where, when, what would I sing?" I stammer, my heart proud and scared at the same time. Jenny and Jason walk in from the kitchen. "Isn't it wonderful?" she says to me as they both sit on the floor next to me. I nod, still stunned.

Reverend Carlos Manual stands, "What a beautiful message from the angels, a true miracle! Maggie, everyone in church has always said you have the voice of an angel. The angels must be listening. But we can't have an announcement at the church. Patrick's painting is undoubtedly about bringing the world together, all faiths, all people. In the first drawing, the angel held a dog in his arms. It's a big message for us all and it has to be told in a neutral setting."

As his mind whirs, Reverend Carlos says, "Maggie, you could sing with the choir from the High School. You could sing that beautiful song we sing in church every year, *Bless the Beasts and the Children*." Everyone agrees it's the perfect song.

Josh pipes in, clearly concerned, "This is wonderful, amazing really, but everyone, we have to remember we must be conscious of the notoriety this will bring the town. We have established ourselves now as a town, not where angels reside, but where everyday people give back in an angel's way. I know for Hannah and our family how hard it was to have the media everywhere hassling us." He puts his arm around Hannah and she leans on his shoulder. I can see the worry written on her beautiful face.

July North speaks for the first time. Her baby sleeps soundly in her arms. "Willie and I have an idea. We have been thinking hard about this. Reverend, I think your idea with Maggie and the High School choir is great. The angels obviously want her to sing. We could announce it on my show again in the town square like last Christmas Eve when Hannah's book came out about the town. I'm thinking a week from this Sunday on my show. I can make it work. Maggie and the choir could sing and we could call it "Songfest For The Angels." No mention of the children's names, of course, but Mayor Willie and I talked about it. He could be my main guest, explain the miracle of what's been happening here. We could have Jumbotrons and Main Street sealed off like we did before. We could show the artwork on the screens. We could draw as much focus as possible on the art, a little girl's speaking for the first time as messages from the angels and get a discussion going of the miraculous meaning to the world. Maybe the angel drawings could tour the country. That way the focus would be taken away from Mystic Bay. We could advertise it as revisiting Mystic Bay and the Songfest. This way, the town will hopefully be spared too much press. What do you all think?"

Guy Benfield speaks up, "Yes, July and Willie, I like this, but *The Mystic Bay Town Crier* will only advertise the show as a *Songfest*. I don't want to write anything that will indicate it's our child who is the artist. There must be complete anonymity for the children. I could have *Dan Pico from the San Francisco Chronicle* here to have the story down and published immediately afterwards to our satisfaction. I could give him a heads up as I trust him completely."

Mayor Willie runs his hand through his grey hair, a worried look on his face. "Yes, we don't want to start a stampede of reporters again, whatever we do. For what it's worth, my intuition says we can do it, but we must make a foolproof plan."

Gabe remarks, " Madam Norma called me and said she feels these will be the only two drawings from our town. This may be just a first call. Perhaps there will be sightings by children around the world. "

Bette almost whispers, "I'm afraid because those paparazzi and tabloids were so awful here to you, Hannah and Gabe."

July continues to calm us all. "Don't worry, Bette. My producers and I will make sure we do it right. We can do this, everyone."

Jack says, "Whatever we do, it has to be slick and promote the message as a one time only thing. July and Willie, you could explain that the sightings were short-lived. How the children have gone back to normal activities. How now we must wait and see if more children everywhere start seeing angels!"

"But that's not really true," Guy says. "Patrick is back to scribbling yet speaking more, and Emma Rose continues to speak."

July says in that calm yet commanding voice of hers, "I know my business like the back of my hand and have ideas swirling around in my head. Don't you worry, please. It will be wonderful."

Josh says, "We don't want our family interviewed at all, but for some reason, if someone happens to invade our privacy or anyone's, for that matter, I think it's best to say, 'Isn't this wonderful. Our town has spread some joy to the world. We hand the baton on to other towns. Who's next?' Maybe have some examples of good things happening like this in other towns."

"Great idea, Josh," says July. Willie concurs. The worry in the room seems to ease. I stare at each person, afraid at the thought of singing for millions. I look at their faces. And then through the talking I hear it again, the rustle of wings. I notice as I go from face to face, some of these folks have mesmerizing, sparkling, starry eyes like Taylors, but the others don't. They glisten and shine in the light, but only when looking directly at me. What's happening to me? Have I stopped hearing trees? I can't see sparkles in Mayor Willie's eyes, or Jack's or his family when they look directly at me. But Hannah, Josh, Gabe, January, and July have the firelight look in their eyes like Taylor. They sparkle; they shine like tinsel on a tree, like glistening sunshine on new fallen snow. The auras are all different...soft yellows, oranges, and blues. Then the song sings through my mind; it's a song for everyone. Everyone heartily agrees, it's the perfect song. We finish our meeting and I excuse myself, desperately wanting to go home and leave before the others. As I go out to the kitchen, Jenny touches my arm and whispers. "How did it go with Brian?"

"Awful," I blurt out. "I have to go. I'll tell you later." I almost run home, splattering my shoes in puddles, wet wind in my face. Home is where I've always felt safe with my two beloved mothers. Home! I'll go to my animals and the pine tree in the backyard. My biological mother means nothing to me. She gave me life, that's all. I take the manila envelope, holding it out before me letting the rain soak in, hopefully ruining the information inside. Brian seemed so proud, gathering it carefully for me. The rain comes down, pouring now as I run. I can't hear the trees anymore but realize I'm crying too hard. I stop by a puddle near my house and listen.

I stand still, my canvas shoes already soaked. Four little yellow roses fall lightly, then land in the water. I look around. There are no rose bushes anywhere in view. They came from the rainy skies. Is this a sign? My tears stop. Only rain wets my cheeks now. I'm not frightened anymore because beloved nature has given me her sign. Go slowly like falling snowflakes to the ground. How beautiful they are, a heavenly gift blown in from a neighboring bush. I must stop and take time to admire the beauty of the earth and not concentrate on my worries, now so insignificant. Angels are calling the children. I start to sing the song I'll sing for the masses, the song I remember, It's the song Mr. Beasley whistled once as he walked the shore with the tide rolling by. *Bless the Beasts and the Children*. It's the perfect song. It's what we're all about in this seaside town with a harbor shaped like the top of a heart. It's what we humans need to do. We must be like knights in shining armor. We are the blessed children and the beasts of the world's greatest hope.

11

Rainy Winds Of Night

Gram and GG are sitting in their recliners when I arrive home. GG's wearing her blue and pink evening attire, aka, her bathrobe. Gram is dressed in her blue sweater and scarf ready for her date with Tim. They both look concerned as they see my face. Taking my wet shoes off on the porch and coat off at the coat rack, I've left the manila envelope on the end of the front porch, knowing the drips from the gutters will soak it through. I don't want GG and Gram to know about the men in Polly Ann's life. King finds my hand and licks it. "What happened with Brian, dear, and the meeting?" Gram gets up and strokes my head. "You're so wet, let me get a towel."

"No, I'm fine, really." Looking at their worried faces, I know I must tell them at least about Jack. Telling Gram what Brian said about all the men my mother is in contact with would hurt her. I'll throw the envelope in the trash when they've gone to bed. My stomach growls; I didn't eat lunch or even have one of Helen's cinnamon rolls. I explain the story Brian told me about Jack Benfield meeting Polly Ann.

"It just can't be Jack. I hope not anyway. It would cause so much angst for Stella, Jenny, and Guy. There's never been any sort of sign of this at all. Wouldn't I have seen something? Wouldn't you two know about it?"

Gram says gently, "Mother, it can't possibly be Jack, even though there was that time Jack dated Polly Ann!" I almost fall off the chair. I've never heard this. Jenny surely doesn't know about this either.

"What? When was this?"

"Oh, Maggie, there was a rift between Polly Ann and Stella before you were born. Stella and Polly Ann were good friends in High School, but then Jack and your mother went out a time or two after Stella and Jack broke up during the summer they all came home from college. It was brief as I recall, but when they got back together, Stella never spoke to your mother again. Polly Ann said Stella wouldn't even look her way if they walked by each other on the street. But Polly Ann didn't try to talk to her either. No, my intuition says no. If that dear Jack thought he was your father, he would have come forward. He's that kind of man. It's never crossed my mind. It's someone we don't know I feel, someone who lives far away. I've always thought that."

"I know you both would tell me if you had a vibe about it. It just can't be him."

GG and Gram have tried to shield me. They tried to make my life so good without a mother and father, and they truly succeeded. I look down and pet King. I don't want Jack to be my father. For me it would be wonderful, but for Jenny and Guy and Stella? No.

Mabel made hot chocolate before she left; I get up and get us each a cup with marshmallows floating on top. Trying to make Brian's information go away and focus on the best news of the day, I sit down, telling them about the meeting and Patrick's latest angel painting and the decision for me to sing one of my favorite songs. How July's planning the event in town square again. GG and Gram cry happy tears to think I will sing for the angels. They chatter like Bubbles does, conjecturing how they want a front row seat. When it's time for me to get ready for my job, I realize I left out the auras of everyone in the room. Should I tell them about seeing golden starlight eyes, and hearing wings rustle? It's best keeping it to myself for now. Maybe I was light-headed, stressed out by Brian, no food all day, and emotionally drained. Now, I'm much calmer. God made sure of that, sending little yellow roses falling around me. My life is good; it doesn't matter about my father. It never has. Has it? No, I have to concentrate on *The Songfest for the Angels* and how wondrous it will be to sing for everyone.

The wedding party has all but gone from the restaurant. It's been a busy Saturday night and I'm thankful for that. No time to obsess about everything Brian said. Jack, Tad, Jenny, and I were so swamped there was no time to talk, although Jenny asked what had happened with Brian. I gave her the brief synopsis of men, leaving out the part about her dad, of course. I watched Jack for a moment while he was working. Do I look like him? Not really, though his mother was Italian, his skin is olive, and his hair is dark like mine. I've thought I looked like a dark haired version of my mother and must have a Mediterranean father. Jenny has Jack's same tall stature, same smile, yet eyes and skin of Stella's Dutch background. But what could he and my mother have been arguing about, I question, walking home in the late night rain. I have an umbrella and find it soothing to walk home smelling the rain, the nourishing water refreshing life around me. Noah is coming by at eleven. Gram will be in bed after her movie date with Tim and GG will be asleep. I'll make him some tea, we'll sit by the fire and I'll try to be unruffled, hoping the emotion won't ruin the romance blooming. I'm perplexed and elated at the same time. Why did Brian pick now to show up? My anger at my mother comes to the surface. Why did she do this to Gram, to GG, and to me? Why couldn't she just tell the truth, then leave, and at least be civil, writing us a card at Christmas, calling now and then. I push back the negativity. The angels want me to sing? I'm not a professional singer; just sang in the teen choir, soloing occasionally. I think of the sparkling eyes of my friends, the sounds of the wings coming from where? What is happening? The angels are calling us now and I'm seeing auras and diamond eyes and hearing wings flutter! Incredible! I stop and listen. Yes, I hear them for sure; I can hear the trees through the melody of rain.

12

Noah's Angel

Noah knows I'm here. He sits at his desk in his bedroom reading over and over the words in the letter. Lorraine found Smarty rummaging through a box on the floor of his Dad's old letters, scattering them everywhere. Ironically, yet meant to be, of course, the bunch she picked up first produced a letter addressed to Marshall Greenstreet, sent to his old New York address, post marked thirty years ago from Mystic Bay. Noah reads the letter again then turns around to see me standing in the corner. It's the first time in his life he has seen me so vividly, his guardian angel.

His mouth opens, he can't speak. Even though I'm seven feet tall, I know I don't scare him, for all his life he's felt my presence. He had an awareness of me sitting by his bed when he was a child, an outline, a transparent glow. But now he sees me clearly, standing taller than most humans with eyes reflecting angel light like all angels. My white robe is cinched with a gold tie. My wings are dimmer to the eye; their purpose takes me traveling with golden shine to each dimension. To me I'm just an angel; to him I'm the comforting glowing presence he remembers. He used to talk to me and tell me his troubles as a child. He wondered who his biological mother and father were and I would help him find the strength inside to wait...wait till he was a grown man to find the truth. It's been almost twenty years since he's needed me like this. He needs me now.

"Hello, Noah," I say with a smile. "I know you're unafraid. I have been beside you so many times and now you can see me fully. It is time you do."

"Francis?"

"Yes, Noah, I'm here for you."

He stands, showing me the letter, but I already know what it says.

> Dear Son,
> I may never know your name but I love you just the same. I held you for a moment when you were born. So sweet and warm you were against my skin. I only gave you up

because I am young and scared and have no money of my own. No one in my life can know about you. Oh how I wish I could be with you. Your father said he would give you this letter when you grow up then maybe you would understand.

    I had a brief love affair with the man who is your father and so you were conceived in love. I will love you always and keep you as a treasure in my heart. You will grow up to be a fine man. Maybe someday you will find it in your heart to forgive me.

Your loving biological mother

13

The Warmth Of The Fire And You

The fire is blazing yellow and gold with blue tipped flames. "Tell me what happened," Noah sighs, sinking into the couch holding my hand. I gaze into his beautiful amber eyes, yet surmise something is wrong. There's a pensive look, a strain in them. He asks again.

"Well, I'll start with the beautiful news. Patrick painted three angels singing. It's astonishing, reminiscent of *The Starry Night* by Van Gogh. Hues of indigo and stars, a watercolor...it's extraordinary!"

"Really? Oh, my God. This really is happening, isn't it?" He stands and I take his hand again. "That's not all, Noah. Patrick says the angels want me to sing." He is lost for words for a moment, then comes to me kneeling. "Maggie Joy, this is why you were named Joy. You are to sing for the angels." He puts his head in my lap and begins crying. Not knowing what to do, I place my arms around him. He lifts his tear-stained face to mine and gives me a kiss on the forehead.

"You're so emotional. It is wonderful, isn't it?" Noah wants to hear all about the meeting and the plans for the *Songfest For the Angels*. I explain it will be a week from Sunday on July's show, and the hesitancy and worry about the media trampling into town again like bulls, almost wrecking the peace of the place, like two years ago. Yet everyone agreed with July, the show must be in the Town's Square again.

"And Brian?" That's all he says, still a look of sadness with a residue of tears on his cheeks. Wiping the rest of his tears away, I hesitate, not wanting to spoil the angel moment. But I begin, relaying how Brian thinks he's found information about men in my mother's life that could lead to my real father. I confess to leaving the soggy envelope on the porch, how I plan to throw it out. I put my head down, explaining Jack Benfield's ties to my mother. He's silent, looking over at the fire's embers finally burning down to a quiet occasional pop. He turns to me, "Will you speak to Jack about this?" His handsome face seems sadder still.

"It seems so unimportant now. I can't even think about it, with the children's extraordinary visions of angels. I'm afraid to ask Jack, afraid it will ruin my relationship with them all if I find out he is my father. Why was he meeting my mother? As much as a gift it would be to have a wonderful man like Jack as my biological father, it could destroy my friendship with Jenny. Gram and GG's psychic vibes say he can't be my father."

Noah stands and goes to the window. Rain falls down the panes in lovely patterns, reflecting the firelight. He turns to me, but something has changed in him. There's sadness now almost unbearable to see.

"What's wrong, Noah?" He comes back, putting his arms around me.

"I'm overwhelmed right now. Things have gotten worse for Dad. I brought a letter to him today and he didn't seem to know who I was. My life's changed, so many things I want to talk to him about and now he's gone."

"I'm sorry." I wrap my arms around him. This beautiful man is so sad. His father's brain has given way to dementia. And my life is astounding and lovely in part, yet feels out of control, confusing like a convoluted dream. Maybe he'd like to find out who his real mother and father are and feels I'm being selfish, not wanting to know the other information Brian surely found.

Before he leaves, Noah looks at me with concern, "Don't throw out the info Brian gave you. I will keep it for you, unopened. You might change your mind. In fact I'm sure you will." He's right, of course, so as we go outside, I find the soaked envelope and hand it to him. He shakes it out, kisses me goodnight, and leaves.

I go back in, lock the door, and turn out the light in the parlor. But before I head upstairs, I sit on the couch looking out the window. King jumps up and I hug him. Tears fall down my cheeks like the raindrops on the windowpane, but King's furry neck dries them away.

14

The Sweetest Of Days

Like a wave of magic, dawn has broken with disappearing grey purple clouds. A line of white blue sky gives way to the golden sun opening up morning's beauty. The birdsong seems louder. My Bishop pine and all of nature's gifts drink in yesterday's rain. I breathe in the clean smell, touching the bark, feeling and hearing the rhythm. The birdsong makes me say to King, "Happy as a lark, I guess, is the expression." Are larks happy? Do all our animal friends and God's nature feel innate happiness? The golden bee lights on a nearby rose bush. I walk slowly to it. Wish I had a magnifying glass. Its wings are feathery, unlike any I've seen, so beautiful, almost angelic. Am I really seeing this?

Taking my cell phone from my pocket, I send a photo of the bee to Noah. I'll have to ask him about the book he talked about logging all the bees in the world. Now he can send this to his father's friend, the entomologist he mentioned. And what about Noah? His text this morning sounded cheery, *"Jogging early. Much to do before I leave. Lunch today Next Door Café 12 to make up to you for my mood? Love, N."*

Of course I text back *"Yes c u then!"* I want to apologize for my insensitivity. It feels good deciding to be totally transparent about what's happening. I'm going to tell him about the trees, about seeing a starry light in the eyes of Taylor, July, January, Gabe, Josh and Hannah...Angel light? That's what their eyes look like, like the angel's eyes in the dream that brought me home. Lord knows Gram and GG have enough to worry about, but I should tell them too. Why am I keeping this to myself? I'm afraid I'm hallucinating. Or am I afraid of the psychic abilities coming on strong?

Mr. Beasley is waiting for me, it seems. He's bundled in a heavier jacket today as the rain brought a cooler breeze. King's breath fogs the air. Mr. B, as I decide to call him, now waves me over to sit on the bench by him. I comply.

"Thanks so much, Mr. B, for coming over at the restaurant. I'm sorry if I embarrassed you in front of my ex-boyfriend. It's a long, pathetic story." Mr. B pets King who looks up adoringly.

"Don't like seeing you unhappy, Maggie. Everything all right now?"

"I'm fine. You hardly know me, yet you came to my aid. You're so nice. Can I call you Mr. B?"

Mr. B smiles. "Of course!" His sunny disposition catches the sunlight. The sun is shining bright and the air suddenly is warmer. I can see seagulls in the sky in his yellow-red wire rimmed glasses. "Mr. B, where do you live?" He pats King and King gives him his paw.

"Not far from here, down by the pier. I so love this town, Maggie. I've got to go but wanted to see you this morning to see if you were okay. You and King take care of each other and have a good day. I'll see you tomorrow, weather permitting." He gets up to leave, but I touch his coat.

"Wait. Um, would you come by for tea one day to meet my great grandmother, Madam Norma and my Gram, Miss Marilyn? We live up Moon Road, Madam Norma's Parlor. My Great Grandmother, GG is the oldest psychic in town and my Gram is a wonderful clairvoyant. I'd love for you to meet them sometime."

"Yes, I'd love that. You are fortunate Maggie. You have people who love you. That's what life's about, isn't it?" Not waiting for an answer, Mr. B says, "Someday you have to call me Neal." He tips his hat and moves on, whistling a tune. I want to stop him and tell him about the angel sightings; about that song *Bless the Beasts and the Children* I'm going to sing a week from Sunday. King and I sit and watch him walk as far down Beach Road as we can until he turns down Sea Scallop Road. Seagulls soar above us; my hair blows free in the slight but cool wind. The smell of the sea and the mild day make me say out loud, "the sweetest of days." With the sounds of lapping waves I can't hear the trees, but I will as soon as we walk up the alley. I start to hum the song for the angels. King looks at me and places his head on my lap. I watch joggers and walkers moving with freedom next to the shimmering sea. Just like the trees, I hum. Angels are calling me; Noah and I are having lunch today. How sweet life is. I put Brian's words to the back of my mind. Today will be a good day. It's time to walk towards home and the trees will welcome us as always. Do angels hear the hum and join in?...How I wish I could hear the angels sing.

—   —

Laurjean sashays like always round the tables with coffee pot in one hand and iced tea pitcher in the other. The café is packed as usual on a Sunday and most patrons are having breakfast. Sunshine Pancakes are flying off Donnie's griddle. People I know call hello. Noah sits waiting for me by the window. He's so utterly handsome; I take in a shallow breath. His hair is swept to one side and, unbelievably, he seems to have his amber eyes only for me! " Maggie, my joy," he says kissing me lightly and touching my hair. I've combed it out long today. "You're so beautiful."
  "You too," I say, meaning it. Noah laughs. "No ones ever said that, but thanks."
  Chris, Laurjean's cute older son, takes our order of the famous pancakes and I take a sip of my coffee, feeling at ease. Chris's eyes have that sparkle in them like the others at the

meeting. I shake my head. Wow, this is bizarre. Am I becoming as psychic as Noah?

"I want to apologize," Noah says, taking my hand. "I was pretty emotional last night. I really don't want to leave again tomorrow morning for book signings. I don't want to leave Dad or you but I have to. There's something else I need to tell you." He has that sad smile again.

"Noah, I'm the one who should apologize. You must think me selfish not wanting to know what Brian found out. Do you think I should? I'm afraid to look, don't want to think about it now. I'd rather think about the angels appearing and about being with you." Oh, God, why did I say that? But Noah takes both my hands in his. "I'm sorry I interrupted you again."

"You are amazing. And I don't find fault with you at all. Look, I thought long about the envelope last night. If and when you want me to look at it all for you, I will. I'll research it for you. It would make me happy to help you. Months, years down the line, whenever you decide...I'll help, okay?"

"You're so great? Thank you."

I sense there's something he wants to tell me. What is it? Something has hurt him deeply. He pulls out a small envelope from his briefcase. Looking around to see if anyone is watching us, he hands it to me.

Seeing that it's postmarked from Mystic Bay thirty years ago, my heart begins to race. I take the letter out of the envelope, looking at his eyes. He nods as if to say, go ahead, read it.

As I read the words, my heart breaks. Noah's biological mother is from here, Mystic Bay. She's saying she's sorry. She'll always love him. Is she implying Noah's dad, Marshall, is actually his biological father? His father had an affair and then adopted baby Noah? Could Marshall have kept this from him all these years? But why? Did Josephine, his mother, know about this? "Noah?"

"I need you to help me, Maggie." From his briefcase he hands me, **One Psychic Summer**, the first in the Connor Diamond series. On the cover, written in gold, is the title, a blue image of the beach and a seaside town in the distance. In white lettering at the bottom...by Marshall Greenstreet, a novel. "Will you read this for me and try to figure out who Sahara is, the heroine in the book? The names have been changed. of course. You can ask your Gram and GG to help if you can't figure it out. It came to me last night that you will be the one to find my mother. Could you interview the ladies you think are in the book on the premise that you're doing research for me for an article I'm writing about my father's life? You can explain his illness; tell them you're my assistant. You will know her, my psychic sense tells me. You will find my mother, you'll see it in her eyes."

15

One Psychic Summer

"While Noah was gone, I read the novel in only three days, late into the early mornings. It began the thirty-year run immortalizing the semi-disheveled hippy-type character endearing to Marshall's readers. Using his intuition and low-key manner, Connor solves the first in the series set in the fictitious town of Sandy-By-The-Sea, California. The town notes the nickname on the sign across the road as you enter the town...*Welcome to Psychicville*, the town's sign says underneath. A good man, and pillar of the community, has gone missing. Connor Diamond, a fresh out of college hippy drifts into town and offers to solve the case. Even the first Chapter made me wish the book would never end.

  Connor Diamond walks into the little fifties diner named Vicky V's. It smells like bacon and eggs. He's starving for a bacon and egg breakfast even though he tried like hell a year ago to cleanse with a macrobiotic type diet. It didn't work; he loves greasy spoon food too damn much. It feeds the soul, he thinks. A pretty, short blonde behind the counter says, "Come on in. Coffee's always on us." Connor likes her right away. Although he'd prefer to drink a nice tea if possible, he doesn't mention it. A mafia type looking guy in a policeman's uniform turns around. Dark curly hair, rugged complexion, but radiating a kind demeanor he says, "Just visiting?"

  Connor Diamond is a little intimidated at first because of the policeman's stature and besides it says 'Chief of Police' on the black and white police car parked outside. Connor is embarrassed and smoothes his rumpled clothes. On his drive across country, he's been sleeping in his car mostly and showering every few days at little cheap motels. He answers, "Just passing through. Want to get to Washington state. It's taken me a month. You know, seeing the country."

  "Chief of Police Barney Freed," the Chief says, offering his hand to Connor. They shake hands. The grip is firm and strong.

  "Connor Diamond. Looking for work to get my next tank of gas filled and then up to those redwoods…always wanted to see 'em. Then onward I go, north then. I don't know where to next."

  Barney Freed gestures for him to sit on the red padded chrome stool next to him and he does.

  "Man, that sounds fun, traveling the country in your car for a month, but I'm hitched to Vicky here and I'd sure miss this pretty woman."

  "Vicky Freed," the cute perky waitress says, holding her hand out. "And we own this place. We have the best food in town…no need to go anywhere else,

Connor. Listen, I know what you could do, stick around. You could help solve the local mystery that's got my good-lookin' hubby here on edge. His best friend went missing two months now and no leads, nothing. Why, he's lost ten pounds worrying. Even the FBI snubbed us, said Rich just left his wife and kid and took off. Would you like to do a little detective work for us? People in this town are scared to talk to Barney about what happened to Rich Stapleton. They're afraid of his witch of a wife, Tessa. She really is a witch and runs their drug store now and I think even my macho husband here's a little afraid of her too, but I'm not, not one little iota."

"Take it easy, Vicky. Connor's just passin' through, not a detective, so let's not bother him, okay? Nice meeting ya though." Barney sighs, gets off his stool, sweetly kisses Vicky across the counter, and takes the last gulp of his coffee.

"I'd like to help," begins Connor. "I'll help you for sure if you might give me a place to stay and a job." Barney and Vicky look at each other and Connor continues, " You see, I know what I look like to you, just a hippy, but I'm smart and intuitive. I can solve TV crime shows and mysteries in books every time. I'd like the challenge. When I drove into town, the sign read Sandy-By-The-Sea Welcome to Psychicville. I assume that means there are some psychics around town. I say that cause my Grandma Donna Diamond, who's one wise psychic lady says it's been passed down to me and I need to use it. I'm well, a touch of a psychic myself."

Reading chapter after chapter of the affable unlikely gumshoe, Connor Diamond, got me hooked. Connor, the young sleuth manipulates the town's timid folks, psychic and not, for information on Rich Stapleton and his non-adoring black-eyed mate, Tessa. He surmises after the first two chapters that foul play is involved, especially after talking to the townsfolk coming in for breakfast, lunch, or just coffee and a donut at the counter. Loveable characters all, they open up to Connor who's learned to be a short order cook, and make eggs and bacon to sheer perfection, thanks to Vicky. He has plenty to eat now and a place to sleep and a shower in the back of the diner. He just asks folks that come in, "Hey, anything exciting ever go on in this place? Hey, I hear Rich Stapleton disappeared. Wow, that's too bad. He owned Big Rich's Drug Store right?"

Engaged in the story, I found Connor grows to like the town. He decides he may never want to leave its shiny coastline with spectacular views. Yet, he's had an epiphany. He now knows his calling; he's a psychic detective and no one is going to talk him out of his newfound profession. So he writes down the information about Tessa and Rich from whomever he's talked to that day. He places the information on the rickety table next to his cot and, like a game of Concentration, he turns the pieces of paper over and over, solving the puzzle of Rich's disappearance. Tessa's one mean woman, that's for sure. She's gotten rid of Rich Stapleton, but where is he? Connor's not sure.yet. And so the story's mystery unfolds.

It's the characters that intrigue me. I'm positive he's put GG in as Rita-Juanita, the town's wisest psychic and her daughter, Karla, a clairvoyant, the spitting psychic ways of my grandmother. Rita-Juanita and Karla surmise Rich Stapleton is indeed alive; they sense it but don't know where he is. The evil wife, Tessa, is too dangerous to discuss. Rita-Juanita told him, "She is powerful and people fear the squint that comes into her black eyes. We all turn away, Connor, we have too. We are, every one of us, intuitive enough to know we can't mess with her." But the two psychics feel sure Rich is somewhere under duress.

Even though he's changed some characters' appearances, Mayor Willie Walin appears in perfect personality as Mayor Dave Mosky, the Palmist. He read Rich's palm years ago. He concurs Rich is alive as he was meant to have a long happy life. But it's the beautiful heroine in the story that's got me psyched, hoping to find the answer for Noah. She's the one Connor falls for, Sahara Rios, the Latin beauty. Which one of the Mystic Bay psychic beauties from thirty years ago captivated Connor Diamond, aka, Marshall Greenstreet's heart as he interviewed her for his first novel? He must have fallen in love with the young woman he interviewed and characterized in the story. Has fiction imitated real life? I know it has.

Another chapter of One Psychic Summer...

> "Her dark hair like midnight reflects bright flecks of star shine. Connor watches the young Latin psychic, Sahara, move, almost floating across her tiny apartment near Main Street. She tells Connor he needs to look in a wooded place. He will find Rich Stapleton there. She doesn't know where though, or how far away. No more clues. That's all. "Please find him, Connor." She loves Rich, she says; she's always loved him. It was torture watching this man she adored marry mean Tessa and have a child. Tears fall down her perfect cheeks. "I don't know which direction to send you. I just know he is alive, Connor. I try to send him messages with my brain, but Rich isn't psychic. I've loved him since I was a girl and he was working at the drug store. When I was sixteen. I

told him I loved him one day. But he just smiled that handsome smile and told me, "Now Sahara, you're young. You go and find yourself a nice boy from school, okay?"

"Mr. Nice Guy, as everyone called him affectionately, didn't get it. He thought I had a teenage crush, but I didn't. I loved him, couldn't he see that? Why was he with that witch, Tessa? Probably because his father, Big Rich, owned the drug store and took Tessa in when she came to town with a heart-wrenching, made-up sob-story about her sorry life. Everyone in town, but Big Rich, who didn't have any psychic awareness, knew she was a manipulative liar, but no one wanted to interfere. Big Rich gave her a job, moved her into their house, and encouraged Rich to take care of her. The rumor was, Young Rich was bewitched. She put some concoction in his drink like Love Potion Number Nine but its' effects went away fast; even before their son Jake arrived. Then, unfortunately, the old man died suddenly and Rich had to take over everything. He was just out of college and yet he managed the drug store so well, I'm sure his father is proud as he watches from heaven. Rich was kind to me, to everyone. Through the years I kept him in my heart and one day about six months ago, I saw him on the beach walking his dog. We were alone, no one in sight. We strolled awhile with our dogs and we starting meeting to walk together. It just happened; we fell in love. It was easy, the real love we found, and one day he didn't fight it. He was miserable with Tessa, he said. She was cruel to their son and he had to leave her, get the poor boy out of harm's way. He had to find the courage. The day he promised he would tell her it was over *was the last time I saw him. The next day he was gone. But I was afraid, Connor, afraid to tell a soul, even Barney, our good Chief of Police. Afraid she knew about me and she would come for me next. I had this overwhelming feeling someone would come to help me, and here you are, Connor! You will help me find him, won't you?"*

Connor felt her arms around him, clinging, sobbing. He wished he would never have to let her go.

As I read I wondered which of the young psychic women could it be that Marshall Greenstreet interviewed years ago and had a love affair with, producing a son? Which one was Sahara? I picture the intuitive women I know who are fifty-ish or just barely fifty now, old enough to be Noah's mother. In the novel is Sahara, Sharon Manuel, the tall dark-haired beauty, the minister's wife? She's so quiet and yet a gifted medium, so centered on caring for the children she babysits. Carlos and Sharon have twin teenage girls and seem happily married. Or could it be Alma Walin, the Mayor Willie's lovely wife and mother of Andy who does Reiki and healing? Or Tina Beaujolais, Tarot card reader, Jason's mom, still with Phil Doherty after years, having a son together but never marrying? All three psychics are beauties with kind natures. Marshall Greenstreets descriptions don't match except for Sharon's Latin beauty. Is that too obvious? Are there other psychics in the town I can't think of? Maybe the woman, the inspiration for the character Sahara, has moved away. It's been thirty years since she posted that letter. How will I find Noah's mother? First, I'll set up interviews with each of these three women. No, I'll catch them each off guard. If that doesn't work, I'll go to GG and Gram for help. Maybe they psychically know the answer already. Maybe they've always known.

16

Smoke And Orange Skies

I smell the cigar smoke first. He's at the end of my bed, looking at me, smiling the dear smile I somehow remember. The smoking cigar is in his hand; he looks younger than his last photographs. I remember his face, his clear bright Irish blue eyes, the funny mustache GG loved. He wears his favorite suit and blue bow tie that hang in his closet still. I feel like I'm looking at someone through a sun-filled rain-washed window.

He speaks in nearly a whisper, "*Maggie, my dear, forgive. Forgive them.*"

Then he is gone like swirling wind blows out the candle on our back porch. My great grandfather has come to me. I must tell GG and Gram. I try to leap out of bed to run out of my room but I wake up. My Great Grandpa Joe has come to me in a dream. *"Forgive them,"* he whispered. Is he speaking of my mother and father? Is he telling me to forgive my parents, people I don't even know?

The afternoon is sunny as I head down quaint Main Street. Tonight there will be a perfect sunset, according the *Mystic Bay Town Crier*. I imagine the sky will be blessed with shades of orange. But now birds are singing, calling each other with songs so unique I marvel, listening to their heavenly design. The sound is much louder than before; it almost drowns out the sound of the trees and bushes swaying to the wind. The sidewalk radiates the heat of the afternoon as I leave The Wizard Wrench Hardware.

Noah and I were on the phone last night for an hour. I told him about the dream. Noah says he can learn from my dream too. Forgiving should always be in our hearts. When I find his mother I will tell him, but I haven't told him anything about the three women until I know for sure. He says he doesn't want to know till he gets home, but I will know today. I feel it. He is on a book tour and calls at night when I get home from work and texts me photos of the places he's been… Chicago, St. Louis, New Orleans and now Los Angeles. I assure him I will speak today to Jack about his meeting with my mother, Polly An. I'll ask him if we will refer to her now by her legal name, Lyla. I've known Jack all my life, I can't be afraid. I didn't tell Noah about the hum of trees yet, but I will. I push that from the clouds in my mind.

Alma Walin is not Noah's mother. With her brown long ponytail down her back, she was warm and welcoming. Her beautiful face lit up remembering the past when I asked about Marshall Greenstreet and her thoughts as a consultant thirty years ago for his first Connor Diamond novel. She put her hand over her heart. She fondly reminisced about the interview with the budding novelist.

"So handsome he was then," she exclaimed. "Even though I was engaged to Willie, I have to admit to a school girl crush on that sophisticated man, a writer from New York, and me just a local girl with abilities that scared me back then."

"Tell me, how did he find you?"

"Our town had a solid reputation. Not a fake among us. He read about Willie and his father, Willie Senior, and their palmistry in a San Francisco newspaper. It gave him the idea, he told us, to write about a psychic detective. Willie introduced us since Marshall asked who else in town was really psychic. He was intently interested in my new-found healing abilities and took copious notes. He paid us for helping him and another healthy amount after it was a best seller. He asked all of us if our relationship with him could remain anonymous and, of course, we didn't mind, at least Willie and I didn't. We knew which of us in town he'd likely interviewed. There were just a handful of us in town thirty years ago. Willie, your grandmother, and great grandma were and still are the most known, but the numbers have grown since then. People with intuitive abilities are drawn to this town now. How wonderful his son is writing an article about his father."

"Marshall is ill and so Noah has finished his last novel for him and is on book tour. He asked me to decipher who in town his dad might have interviewed. I tried to use my own limited intuition without asking my Great Grandmother or Gram. He would love to meet you and wanted me to get some notes ready."

" I feel so badly. Marshall is ill. He came in to the store when he moved back here with his wife, Josephine, who was so very ill then. He looked old and wasn't well himself, Willie and I concluded. I offered my services, but he refused. He said his wife didn't believe in psychic healing and so I never met her or helped him, unfortunately. If Noah wants me to visit him and see what I can do, I will, of course." Alma was sincere and I thanked her for her help, telling her I would give her kind offer to Noah.

Her eyes reflected memories of a long ago chapter of her life. Noah said I would see the emotion in her eyes, but I didn't. Sharon Manuel is babysitting Emma Rose today. I will stop by there after seeing Tina. It's hard to believe it's one of these last two women. However, there could be someone else in town, but whom? I want to talk to GG and Gram, but not now, I want to see if I can find out on my own like Noah thinks I can.

Hannah is putting a sale sign outside her store. We exchange hellos and I tell her I'm interviewing psychics in town for Noah's article. She tells me her family's never met Marshall Greenstreet. We talk for a moment about the wonder of the children's angel sightings. Her eyes seems to shine a little more as I ask her, "Hannah, since the children have seen angels, I wonder if I could ask you a question about your book, **The Town with the Angel Vibe**?"

Hannah gets a far away look to her eyes and I wish I hadn't asked so I say, "I don't want to pry."

"No, go ahead, Maggie. Ask away." She seems sincere and so I just say what I'm thinking.

You wrote all those lovely stories in college. Did you ever see angels yourself in dreams, perhaps because I had a dream just a few months ago? In the dream an angel told me to move home again to Mystic Bay. I wondered if you had that experience too?"

Hannah looks at me, her eyes reflecting that beautiful light again, and something else too. There's relief there and in her whole demeanor now. "Yes, only my family knows this. But yes, I saw angels as a child, Maggie. I saw lovely angels in my dreams."

The trees hum near the sidewalk as I say goodbye to Hannah and head toward Tarot & Tea. Wow, Hannah saw angels in dreams. Perhaps many times, I'm sensing. This is a story I wish I could hear more about. My mind goes back to the task at hand, "Help me, God, help me sense if Tina is the one. I open the door to find Jason's diminutive grandmother, Ethel Marie, in the exact location I always see her. She's reading for someone and their gray and white heads are together, lost in conversation and cards. They're sitting at the antique table with two comfortable chairs in the back of the charming store with it's lovely china and cast iron teapots, and cups from around the world. Different teas line the shelves and there is always a pot brewing for customers. Tina lifts her beautiful blond head when she sees me. "Oh Maggie, I can't wait for the wedding. I hear Helen is making your maid of honor dress. Did you see it yet?

"Helen went shopping and found something she wants me to see. I'm going over to her house when I have time. She says she found an absolutely gorgeous shocking pink chiffon. She's in heaven since you know how she loves pink. Really, it's so kind of her." Tina comes over to me and gives me a hug. She holds my hands and steps back, looking at me.

"And I hear you have a handsome new beau. What's he like, Noah, I mean, the young man you're dating?" Tina looks so beautiful to me. Jason has her soulful brown eyes, her skin, her smile, her high cheekbones. I see Noah in her eyes; they're his eyes too. Why didn't I see it before? There was sadness as she said his name.

Her eyes glisten as I tell her. "He's a great guy, Tina. I've never dated anyone like him before." She hurriedly changes the subject, offering me the brewed, spiced Rooibos Ruby Red Chai, and I sip it while she helps a tourist select tea. I watch her move across the store almost gliding, mannerisms akin to Sahara's in the novel, **One Psychic Simmer.** What could the story be? Did her family know? I know in my heart of hearts they didn't. But she is still in love with Phil Doherty. Why didn't they marry? It must have happened while she and Phil weren't seeing each other. Phil is twenty years her senior. Does he know? Noah will figure out how to proceed. I buy a Queen Elizabeth English Breakfast tea for GG and Gram. I hug Tina; our goodbyes are filled with excitement for Jenny's and Jason's upcoming wedding. Her misty-eyed look follows me out the door. With my psychic understanding I can see her eyes are remembering Marshall Greenstreet, a man she once loved. Her eyes are also remembering Noah, remembering heartbreak. How sad I feel for her, to not know him all these years, the man I'm falling for, Noah Connor Greenstreet, her son.

17

The Rose

I'm walking fast towards home down Moon Road. My tears fall like raindrops. As I left Tina's store, my heart ached for Noah and for Tina. Why wouldn't Marshall tell him the truth? Why keep it from him? I need to go to the back yard to my tree and think about how to tell him. What words will be best. "Tina Beaujolais is your mother, Noah. She is so sad." No, that's not the way to say it, but how? How will I tell him? I must find the gentlest of words.

The door is closed to the parlor with an "In-Session" sign on it. A car is parked out front. I head out the kitchen to the yard. GG seems asleep in the bench glider, King's head upon her lap as usual. But is she sleeping? I panic for a moment running to her. King gets up, bewildered. But GG lifts her curly white head; her sunglasses reflect the sunshine like Mr. B's sunglasses do.

"Hello, Maggie Joy. What is it? What's wrong?" I get on my knees, my head in her lap like King would do.

"I don't know what I'd do without you."

"Oh dear, this old lady's not going anywhere. Not today anyway," she assures me, petting my head.

Looking up at my wise and witty great grandmother, I finally smile. "I'm not done with you yet GG."

"Darling," she laughs, " I was just thinking about it while looking at our beautiful roses. We'll all meet you one day, your Great Grandpa Joe, Gram and me. We'll meet you a long time from now in the center of a lovely rose. We'll take in the fragrant beauty together...that's how I see parts of heaven."

"That's so beautiful, GG. You always have such lovely words for me to ponder. I have to tell you though, he came to me, Great Grandpa Joe; he came last night in a dream. He was smoking a cigar and he had on his brown suit and bow tie, looking like he was about fifty. He said, "Forgive them." I know he was speaking of Lyla and my father. I've decided I need to call her by her legal name now. And whoever my father is, well, I forgive him too. I guess it doesn't really matter, for I have a good life without them."

"Oh, what a wise man my Joe always was. We must forgive others for our own soul. I needed to hear that today; I've been so distraught about it for so long. We can't control others' behavior but we can learn from them. Your mother was troubled then. I fear she may be troubled still. Perhaps we should write her another letter, telling her we will always love her and miss her. It's been too long since we tried and you know how your Gram stuffs in down deep, but the reality is, her heart aches for her. Maybe that could help her. Marilyn is so hurt she won't talk about it anymore. Yet, you are her shining light, and mine. Life includes sadness, Maggie, like falling raindrops, but between those raindrops there's always light and space and beautiful times...look at all we have. We have each other." She looks down at King. "And we have our animal companions who give us so much. And now the angels are calling...and you will sing that beautiful song for them! It's a sign for us to remember the life we have been given. So let's try to reach out to Lyla. The time is nigh."

"Yes, GG. I'll write her a letter myself. Noah said if I need it, he could get her address from people he knows in the entertainment business. It's time. I'm a grown woman. If she doesn't answer back, then we'll have tried, at least. I do feel forgiveness now. I didn't realize before how much anger and fear I had. Great Grandpa Joe came to me in a dream to help me find the answers that were always there."

I sit by GG now and hold her hand. King finds a place to settle under the tree, its hum brings a lullaby now. GG's eyes close. She's napping again. In my letter to Lyla, I'll ask if she'll come see us or perhaps we'll meet her somewhere, to put closure on this for me, for GG, and especially for Gram. I realize now if she has problems, like GG feels, then she's coping with life the only way she can. Maybe she didn't want to live in a psychic town. Maybe she didn't want to be the different one in the house. Maybe she didn't want to have children and feel trapped. Maybe, maybe. What are the answers? They're her answers, not mine.

The seaside sky will soon appear orange as the sun starts it's climb down to the sea, signaling my time to go to work. My cell rings, interrupting the quiet moment. Picking my cell up, GG lifts her head and remarks, "There's been another sighting... angels have called another precious child."

After I've listened to Hannah's message, I smile at GG. "Yes, GG, you're so right. This time a boy with a visual impairment has had a dream; the angels have given him a song for him to play on a piano for us. He says it's a song for the world!"

Gram comes out of the house, down the back steps to us, and sits on the bench glider by GG. "What's happened? I tell her the news. Gram puts her hand on my shoulder. "Wow, this is remarkable, really. Oh, angels, how I've always loved them. I've always wished to see one. But now children are seeing them and angels have sent us a song!"

"Gram, Great Grandpa Joe came to me in a dream last night. His message said, "Forgive them." He meant I was to forgive Polly Ann and my father. I'm going to write Polly Ann but address her as Lyla because she has chosen to change her name. With your blessing, I will write her a letter. I will ask her to please reconnect with us, if only by letter if she wants. What do you think?"

Gram gets a look in her eyes, a look I saw in Tina's eyes. It's that look of heartbreak, so hard to see. "Yes, Maggie. Do it. We must move on and contact her again. Yes, it's time."

I hug my grandmother and great Grandmother, knowing I can't tell them about Tina and the miracle of Noah's dog finding her letter. Also, I can't tell them about the starry eyes of our friends or the sounds of wings. I know my perception is growing stronger or else I'm going absolutely bananas. In my mind I picture the eyes lit with star shine. And then I picture the most lovely thought of heaven I've imagined, meeting those you love who have passed away; meeting them in the center of a beautiful rose.

18

The Wiley Ways Return

The angels must be working overtime, because I open the front door to leave for work and standing there are Jamie Bond and Tim Thayer, quite the unlikely pair. I introduce them, but the always polite and distinguished Tim Thayer says, "We've just met at the door, thank you, Maggie. I've assured Mr. Bond here that King will not hurt him; however, he prefers to stay here on the front porch."

I call to Gram and she comes and greets Tim and Jamie. Jamie looks somehow put together in a clean tee shirt and jeans and remarks, "Uh ladies, you look different. You looked like witches before."

"Young man," exclaims Tim, "these are the loveliest ladies in all of Mystic Bay." Tim is being extremely nice, even though I can tell he finds Jamie's remark apprehensible.

"Sorry, I meant, you look better."

But dear Gram pipes in, ignoring Jamie's remark. "Oh Tim, this is the young man I was telling you about who needs a job. I think he would be a wonderful asset to any business." Tim looks Jamie over with a wry eye. "Hmm, really."

Jamie blurts out. "Yeah, these ladies with the scary dogs and cat made me see the light. I mean they're giving me money, but that's what I came about. I feel bad taking your money. Like, you guys are old and your daughter here's a spinster, Elena says. You gotta be hurting if you have to hold séance's and stuff. I don't need the money. I applied at GoMart in Riverton and a couple of gas stations. I got my unemployment check coming in so when I get a job, I'll be able to help with Emma Rose. I don't want that big ole angel flying to my apartment with that dog and freaking me out. So, like I said, thanks, but no thanks. Can I keep the money you gave me though 'cause I already spent every friggin' dollar? Sorry."

I don't want to be late for work but can't help staying. I put my hand over my mouth trying to hide the smile. Tim looks astonished as I think he's never witnessed the results of two psychic ladies' wiles in action. He arches an eyebrow.

Gram bursts with enthusiasm. "Oh Jamie, I am so happy for you. You are really doing such a good job!" She gives him a hug. "Yes, I'm glad the money came in handy, and no, King won't come now, although he was really missing you."

TO CATCH AN ANGEL

Jamie looks like he wants to run but stays put. And then the strangest thing happens. In all my years, my ears never thought they'd hear Tim Thayer say, "Why, young man, I run the Farmers' Market every Saturday and Sunday behind my store, Mystic Bay Cheese and Wine. It's on Sea Scallop Lane. You need a job? Why, I could use a young man with a lot of energy to help with the loading and unloading from the trucks. Starts at eleven an hour. I could use your help, if you're interested in hard work, that is," Tim offered.

I look at Gram and she winks at me.

"Hey, yeah, that would be cool, thanks. Uh, you don't have a big dog, do ya or black cats?"

"Why no, young man, just Muffy, my tiny Chihuahua. She comes with me to work and is the sweetest little dog this side of town." By now King is at the door with GG following behind him with her walker. Gram puts her hand on King and he halts but eyeballs Jamie. Jamie's wide-eyed yet looks at GG. My hand is still covering my mouth. Me, a spinster at twenty-six! It's amazing. Did Mr. James Bond ever hear of the Woman's Movement?

"Hi, Grandma Norma," he says to GG. GG blows him a kiss. Obviously, she's been using her psychic vibes, for something's up. Grandma Norma? This is funny. All of a sudden, I realize Jamie's been in communication with Gram and GG. When was it? Was it by phone or did he come over while I was at work? Jamie looks at the dog and then at Tim and says, "When can I start?"

It's an unlikely lovely pairing like Champagne and hot dogs, but a real job for Jamie. GG and Gram have done a wonderful thing. After I say goodbye to all and walk down a few steps, Tim Thayer, the most quiet gentleman I know, says, "You know Jamie, James Bond has always been my favorite character in books and movies. I always wished I were as suave and debonair as he. What a very cool name you have! A real hero's name!" King lets out a huge bark and I turn around, but Jamie is still there, sweating for sure but still there!

19

Once Upon A Dream

The sun is setting in an orange foggy swirl. Everyone in Jack's By the Sea is all atwitter talking about *The July North Show* airing tomorrow night. Jack will shut the restaurant down for a special party afterward to celebrate. Only those of us who planned the event know the three children have encountered angels. The information has spread through town and advertising on TV that it's a songfest for the angels, a celebration of the town's angelic contributions to society, they all think. Everyone congratulates me upon hearing I will sing on national TV. I try not to think about it. With the Mystic Bay High School choir and a San Francisco Symphony quartet accompanying us, well, how can I mess up?

I haven't had the heart to ask Jack about his meeting with the woman I have decided to refer to as Lyla Jasmine. It is her name now, and we should respect her wishes. I concentrate on the excitement with the Sunday Songfest, yet little do the crowd and TV viewers know how extraordinary it really is. Another child has a song given to him by the angels. He's just moved to town with his family. His father plays violin in the San Francisco Symphony and will be in the quartet. Benny Chen, the gifted ten–year old, is legally blind but plays the piano well. The angels came to him in a dream, he told his parents. The melody they gave him that night is a message from above. Hannah told me this song will bring tears to the eyes of all those who listen. "It's mesmerizing," she said. Mesmerizing like her eyes, I wonder.

Noah is driving home from LA tonight, home late as the San Francisco airport is fogging in. He wants to hear the news about his biological mother in person. "I want to be with you holding me when you tell me," he said on the phone. My heart aches for him.

Tad is dressed in a suit and tie. "Tad, you look great. Dressed up for a party?" I smile at him.

"No, Jack gave me the manager position yesterday. I'll be following him, job shadowing him now. He's been so great to me. Now he wants to scale back, and Jenny and Guy have their own careers so I get this opportunity. Still I'll barkeep once in a while."

"Wow, I'm so happy for you. You have a way about you, Tad. You'll be super at it, but hey, where will Missy sit?" I say it realizing I should keep my filter filtered. "I'm sorry," I say sincerely.

"It's okay, Maggie. I broke up with her. The way she acted towards Noah and you when you fainted really burned me. She kinda stalked me anyway. I need a woman like you, kind and beautiful, too." He laughs. "Got any sisters?"

"Thanks, Tad. You know what? I have a darling cousin, Marcy. She'll be up here from San Jose for Jenny's big day. You can meet her then."

"Sounds like a plan." He walks away with a lighter step and a plan brewing for a good life. He'll have more stability and still surf on his days off. That's his way to peace, and he'll be more financially solvent. I'm happy for the nice guy whose father disowned him for what, for having a job and loving to surf? I do feel blessed to have GG and Gram. I almost run into Jack as he comes around the corner. I hear Mario singing a song loud and strong. He sounds almost like Andrea Bocelli. Maybe he should sing instead of me the song for the angels. I feel a lump of fear form in my throat...what if my voice cracks?

"Maggie, can I talk to you a moment?" Jack looks serious.

"Sure," I say, afraid of what's next. We walk into his office and he shuts the door behind him. "Maggie, there's something I need to tell you." Oh God, I feel lightheaded again but hang onto the desk chair. "Sit down, please," he gestures with a sad smile on his kind face."

The fog hasn't lifted. I toss and turn, worrying about Noah driving in from LA. What time will he arrive? After midnight? My mind drifts as I hear the trees hum through the slit in the opened window. Breeze comes in cold. How will he react to the news? I see his eyes, his mother's eyes. Drifting off trying to imagine I'll hear his car come down Moon Road past my house, I try to remember everything Jack said about my mother so long ago. I sat down, then blurted out, "Are you my father? Brian, my ex-boyfriend, said he had her followed and you met with Polly Ann at the Paradiso Hotel." I so wanted to cry but held back, knowing my tears would flow like rain off the roof.

Jack began the story. Stella asked him to contact Polly Ann and ask her who my father was. Jenny wanted me to finally know the truth, to get answers. Stella wouldn't talk to my mother herself because Jack and my mother had a brief affair in college. Just like Gram said, it was right after he and Stella broke up for a while.

Jack had such melancholy on his face when he said, "Jenny has taken the news well. I was a fool to hurt Stella, but I cared about Polly Ann too, then. When you're young, you make mistakes and all throughout life, too. It was brief and long ago, Maggie. I'm sorry you found out that way. Jenny is adamant we help you find your father." He looked out the office window at the fog and ocean for a moment, then he turned to me. "I'm sorry I met with her now because she wouldn't tell me who your father was. I explained how you, your Gram, and Norma are so hurt, but she was rigid. She still has big problems, I think. Money hasn't helped her. She never realized how lucky she was to have you all. I truly wish I could tell you it's me, but I'm not your father. We stopped seeing each other a year before you were born. You are a fine young woman and any man would be proud to be your dad." He walked over to me and I held the tears back as he put his arm around me. "Don't be upset with us, please. You mean so much to all of us."

I'm not upset with them, of course, but it makes me sadder still. I fall asleep again and dream of Great Grandpa Joe and his cigar smoke and then the scene changes to the past... ten-year-old me flying with the dream angel who called me home. I'm aware I'm dreaming. It's a recurring dream from childhood. This blurry dream is back again, the dream when I first saw those amber eyes, when I first saw Noah. Dream angel and I flew far above, like airplanes looking down at the lights of towns scattered below. Our destination in what seemed a nanosecond was New York City. I remember the way the Empire State Building lit up with colors and all the tall buildings welcomed us with bright lights and neon signs. His angel's wings slowed down and we glided to a stop at one of the lighted windows of an apartment building. I was suspended in air, holding the angel's hand, looking in. An older boy was standing at the window looking at me too. He smiled. He had big brown eyes. The fateful dream ended. In the dream, the boy is the man I met just weeks ago. My eyes open and I'm awake now. It was so long ago I'd forgotten, but it's come again, the dream I totally forgot about. Noah said he remembers where we met. Does he remember we met once upon a childhood dream?

20

I Run To Him

My night with Noah has been the most magical night of my life. Just like he predicted, I waited by the window till I saw him drive by our house half past midnight, then I drive to his house near the speed of light.

"I remember," I whisper as he takes me in his arms and carries me to his room. He opens his bedroom door to the outside patio as the fog swirls and the cold night begs in. With tears of joy, he tells me of his guardian angel, Francis, and how he always calmed his fears when Noah was a child. How one night Francis told him to wait by the window and he waited and saw me with my angel for a moment at his window.

"I remembered your beautiful face, Maggie." I'd forgotten that night twenty years ago until a few days after we met. And when I remembered, I thanked Francis even though I couldn't feel him near.

"All my young life," Noah says, "Francis would appear, his glowing outline calming my fears. He would tell me everything would be all right and I'd find the answers when I was grown. You see, I didn't understand why the subject of who my biological parents were was forbidden in my house. My father told me long ago it would hurt Mother deeply to talk about it, and so I never asked. When I found the letter, I prayed for Francis to come again. I hadn't seen his winsome presence or heard his voice in years, but this time he appeared instantly. For the first time I was able to see him in all his magnificence."

Awestruck by his story, I hesitate to tell him about Tina, but he holds me.

"Tell me, tell me now about my mother." I tell him she is Tina Beaujolais and how her sorrow was so clear in the tears in her eyes. They are his eyes, I tell him. He says he plans to go to her. He hopes someday Jason will be told the truth. But it will be Tina's call when. It will be all right, Francis foretold. There will be bumps and slow moving walks forward, but time will help. Noah will wait to speak to Tina since Jason and Jenny get married in a few weeks. He's waited so many years to know the story; why didn't his father tell him the truth? Noah's psychic abilities perceive his dear mother Josephine must have found out. That's why she insisted they move here. With loving kindness, she wanted Noah to meet his biological mother after she died. But the plan didn't work. Marshall's dementia escalated. "My life has changed so much here. My father is indeed my biological father and Tina is my mother? What is the very story of my life? Now, I will finally have the answers I've yearned for."

"I know in my heart it's a love story, Noah. For your father is a good person and so is Tina. He put his love for Tina in the book, brief but heartfelt; Connor's unrequited love for Sahara."

"They must have had an affair while he interviewed the psychics in town, though he'd recently married my mother. I wonder how that could be, they were always so happy. But I'm trying not to judge."

"That's like my mother and Jack's relationship. He told me he cared about her, yet he still loved Stella. How strange love is sometimes, the way it works."

"Francis says not judging others is a hard lesson, but necessary for a wonderful life."

"That thought makes me think. I've been judging my mother my whole life, making her the bad guy. I try to think of her good points and, of course, I can't think of any. I don't know her."

"Maggie, you will figure it all out one day, who your father is and why it happened the way it did. I just know it."

We lie listening to the night sounds. The bigger dogs are snug in dog beds. Murphy and Nursie have joined us now, cuddling in the covers. Outside I hear Noah's trees hum. It's then I decide to tell him the truth...how I hear the hum of life in the trees outside, bending in the foggy night, sipping in moisture. But Noah's abilities have escalated like GG's and he beats me to it. "I know what you are going to tell me, Maggie. When you told me how drawn you are to nature, trees especially, I had a vision of you listening, listening to the trees. You hear them somehow?"

"Yes," I say, astonished at his psychic vibes, "I hear the trees hum, Noah, their sounds of energy, their life."

"Extraordinary! This is a gift from heaven! They're speaking to you, aren't they?"

"I don't know. It's just a comforting hum, a vibration, but it's escalated, the birds are flying nearer, and there's something else, something I haven't told Gram and GG because, well, I'm worried I'm hallucinating."

"What is it, Maggie? Tell me, please."

"Do Francis's eyes shine a golden starry light like the angel's in my dream?"

"Why, yes, yes, they do, as a matter of fact. They're mesmerizing."

"Well, mesmerizing eyes like that? I've been seeing the same light in the eyes of our friends when they look directly at me. I see starlight and auras. I saw an aura around you once. I heard the rustle of wings too. It's all happened since I came back to town, since the children saw the angels."

"Whose eyes, who has these stars in their eyes, Maggie?"

"I see angels' light in the eyes of July, January, Josh, Gabe, Taylor Msumba who works with Hannah, yet dimmer in Hannah's and Chris Whitefeather's. Do you think I'm going crazy?"

Noah holds me tight. "No, Maggie, I think my mother was right. There are angels here, living as humans among us. Maybe others suspect, but keep the knowledge to themselves. What a wonderful town we live in where angels just might live as humans. It's the town I've grown to love through your eyes. Our angels brought us together long ago. We were meant to be. And now they are calling the children, these precious children from Mystic Bay. They are calling you too. They want you to know."

"But why now? Why me? This town, this moment in time?" I can see he's thinking the same thing.

"It may be you were meant to have this ability, this gift, all your life. My theory is it may help you in your work with your students. I can see Francis but why? There are many stories of people seeing angels as they help them in times of need. These stories are from across the world, but I've never read anything about anyone encountering them as friends, except in fictional stories like the novel insinuating Hannah and Gabe were angels. It may be we aren't meant to ask why!"

My heart is overflowing with love for Noah. I can tell him anything. I've just told him the very secret I've told no one else. "You're my angel," Noah says as he kisses me and we fall into the wonder of our love.

21

The Last Chapter Of One Psychic Summer

Noah sees me in his father's office. He's surprised I'm here. "Francis, I'm so glad to see you. I'm in love with Maggie, and truly excited about finding Tina, yet nervous too. But you know all this, don't you?"

"I do," I say gently.

"I'm here to read the last chapter of Dad's first novel again, but I gave my copy to Maggie. Look at all the shelves of his favorite classics from Dickens to Twain. This one shelf is devoted to all his Connor Diamond novels. Every one of them is here, even the newest ones, but I can't find **One Psychic Summer**."

Lorraine walks in the office with his dad. "Mr. Greenstreet and I are going to take a walk around the front yard and look at the angels," the kind, short, and strong companion says to Noah. She can't see me. Looks right through me in fact. "He wants to be by the angels."

"Dad, do you know where your copy of **One Psychic Summer** is? It's not on this shelf. I gave mine away and I need it, Dad."

"I send a thought to his father hoping he will receive it. His incredible mind still can feel emotion, still remember the past sometimes. "Josephine gave it back to me for safe-keeping." Marshall lets go of Lorraine's hand and walks to the desk, opening the bottom drawer. There the book sits, looking worn, but still intriguing with the scene of the imaginary seaside town on the cover. He hands it to Noah. "You keep it now." Then he takes Lorraine's hand again and they start to walk out the door. Marshall turns back looking at me. "See you soon, Angel," he says.

Noah sits on the desk chair looking at the book, then looking at me again.

Lorraine explains, "Oh, Mr. Greenstreet's been talking to spirits or angels all day, Mr. Noah. He sees them, he really does." Tears form in Lorraine's eyes. They walk out toward the front door, her hand holding his.

"He saw you!"

"Yes, it's all right." I feel for Noah. He knows what the discovery of the book means. His father's time to leave is coming soon. "They'll be together again, Noah. It's their love story. There were rough roads in the beginning and then the love, the melting of two hearts happened, and they had you... their precious son." Noah's tears come down. His intuitive abilities will help him now. He knows he will find the answer in the book. Why his father had the affair, the very reason he was born.

Connor Diamond strolls in to Big Rich's Drugstore. There she is, standing at the counter in all her evilness, the lady referred to by all he's met as the "witch," Tessa Stapleton. Her slit-black eyes penetrate his very soul, but Connor Diamond isn't afraid of her. His Grandma Donna did a good job raising him. She always said, "You're a gift to me and someday you'll use your psychic twist for the world, Connor. Remember, don't live scared."

"Mornin, Mam," he says in his polite way. It's the only way he knows how to be.

"Hello," she says, begrudgingly looking him up and down. Connor knows he's still quite a rumpled, hippy-looking kind of guy. But he's clean and has his Vicky V's shirt on and some brand new jeans. His hair is long and tied back in a pony tail. She clearly doesn't like hippy types and that makes Connor really glad.

"Since you're a lady (he coughs), can you recommend a nice perfume for my new girlfriend, Sahara Molina? You know her? Man, she's one pretty girl!" Connor knew that would tick off Tessa and he loved rubbing it in. Now he'll get the clue he needs. How? He'll see it by watching her evil face.

"She's your girlfriend? Ha!" She laughs one of those 'Wicked Witch of the West' laughs and points to the back wall of the store. "There's some cheap cologne back there."

"Why did you laugh like that? She's a nice girl."

"By your shirt I can tell you're working for that bitch, Vicky and her jerk husband. Well, she's just like Vicky. I can say that 'cause I own this place, hippy. With my husband picking up, taking that damned old dog and leaving my kid and me, well, this place is mine, got it? I can say whatever the hell I want."

"Yeah, I got it, lady, but one more thing. Where'd your husband go?"

She has a look in her eye as she turns her head to the northeast just for half a second before she answers him.

"Damned if I know and don't care, so why you asking? It's none of your business, you hippy do-nothing. Why don't you go somewhere else? Go to that little girlfriend of yours. She tried to steal my husband, so you better watch out for her!" He's unnerved Tessa. His psychic twist tells him she's not really a witch, just one mean ole woman.

"Thanks so much for your help. I can't wait to meet Rich; sounds like Mr. Nice Guy!" Connor says politely. "Have a nice day." He turns and walks to the door. He turns around again, noting Tessa's mouth opened in astonishment. "I'll be back with a Big surprise for you!" With that he walks out the door into the sea air and sunshine. Yep, it worked. Rich Stapleton is alive like Miss Rita-Juanita and Miss Karla knew, like Sahara had predicted and Mayor Dave Mosky was sure of. Rich Stapleton is northeast of here in the woods, hours away. Her eyes showed it all. He'll get Barney, Dave, and Sahara and go searching. They will find him. Connor's psychic twist, the way to measure miles in thought, like Grandma Donna taught him, will lead the way. He'll find Rich all right, but hurt, ill, or something.

The drive is beautiful into the mountains of northern California. With Dave Mosky's new red jeep, they drive the highway for an hour, then onto the back roads towards the east where private property is preserved just north of the San Raphael State Park. His abilities are in tune now with the game. Tessa's head turning toward the place where she had taken her husband was as clear as

TO CATCH AN ANGEL

day. How did she manage to do it? They would find the answers. Connor could measure as the crow flies how far he needed to go. Barney is driving Dave's jeep as fast as the Checker Cab in Chicago he took once. The dirt roads are bumpy but not hard to drive. His psychic keen sense of direction is working now. "Turn to the north," he says when they get to a fork in the road. They drive one more hour up and down the private roads with decrepit signs of No Trespassing. And then they come upon an area that seems to have a path, "Stop," says Connor. And for a few minutes as they stop, Connor gets out of the car listening, smelling, and tasting the air, using all his senses as Grandma Donna taught him. He turns his head to the east once more. "The rest we must do on foot," he exclaims. The paths are old and worn. "He's near," Connor tells them. Barney, Dave, and Sahara get out of the jeep. "This way," Connor points. "Start shouting, everyone start calling his name."

"Rich, Rich Stapleton, where are you," Dave calls. Barney shouts, "Rich, it's me, Barney. Rich, where are you?" But Sahara can't speak. She's too emotional, leaning on Connor's arm, holding his hand, following his every step. Dave and Barney take a path off the main one, walking to the west, and Connor and Sahara move south toward a stream they can hear rippling. They hear Barney and Dave calling. Connor gives a loud whistle and he and Sahara see an old furry dog come barking out of the woods. It's a happy bark. "It's Amber, Rich's dog!" Sahara shouts, now laughing, bending down, "Amber where's your daddy?"

"Amber, show us the way," Connor says, petting the dog.

Barney and Dave come their way hearing them talk to Amber. The dog trots back through the woods. There's a rough path of just torn down old branches and grass. "Over here," calls a weak voice. And then there he is, Rich Stapleton sitting with his back up against a tree, next to a very old man. "I'm here, I'm here. We're here." The old man looks up. A real mountain man he is, scruffy beyond anyone Connor's ever seen. But something is wrong with Rich's leg. It's *in a makeshift splint. Sahara almost flies to him first.* "Rich, Rich are you all right? You've lost so much weight. What happened to your leg? Are you okay?" *Sahara throws her arms around him and starts crying. Amber the dog barks her happy call.*

"Yeah, I'm okay." *Barney and Dave get down on their knees and Barney examines his leg.* "What happened, man? Did Tessa do this to you?" *Everyone is ignoring the old man, but Connor's not. Connor sees the old man's surprised expression turn to sadness.*

"I woke up in these woods, my leg had been broken. This great guy, Gus, found me. He's lived here in these woods for a long time now. He's kinda hard of hearing and can't speak. He traps and eats off the land. He's been here years from what I can tell. He's kept us safe and warm in that lean-to there and made us food. Rabbits and squirrels and berries and fish; what-ever he can get. How long have I been here?" *Rich seems a little dazed. Connor thinks it's a miracle the guy survived. If the man Gus hadn't found him, he would have been a gonner.*

"Over two months," *Barney says now.* "Man, it's been rough. The FBI said you just took off so they wouldn't help us. This fellow here is Connor. He came to town a few weeks ago, got clues from all the psychics in town and found you himself with his amazing psychic abilities. He says the town folk gave him the clues. Did Tessa do this to you?"

"Yeah. I told her I wanted a divorce and she hit me over the head with the frying pan. It's the last thing I remember. We were sitting at the kitchen table. My son Jake was at his aunt's. I wanted it quiet when I told her I was leaving and taking Jake. Is Jake all right?"

"Yes, he's living at his Great Aunt Dorothy's now. Tessa claims he's too much for her to handle."

"Oh God," *cries Rich.* "I didn't know how I was going to get home and here you are. Gus here shook his head no when I asked him if anybody ever comes this way. Thanks to you all and, Connor, thank you."

"You're very welcome, sir." Connor is pleased as can be. The man Rich is such a good man, you can tell. Sahara is overwhelmed, crying and laughing at the same time. It breaks Connor's heart a little bit. For Sahara is his dream girl.

"Sahara, you're all right? "

She nods and clings to him. "I was so worried Tessa had done something to you. I knew you wouldn't leave Jake or me. Everyone knew that." Her head is buried in his shirt.

"And to think you, Connor, used psychic ways to find me!"

As we take Rich and his dog Amber home, Connor is pleased with his calling now. A psychic detective he'll be. Won't Grandma Donna be thrilled! He has to leave town now. His crush on Sahara is over; it's got to be. She's hugging her man and crying and stroking his head. Sahara and Connor had a brief interlude, a kiss one night on the beach, just a sweet moment in time. But she loved someone else. Connor surprises himself, because he knows he truly is happy for her.

Barney is ecstatic he has his best friend back. "Man, am I going to get Tessa for this. I'm gonna arrest Tessa as soon as we get back!"

The mountain man Gus refused to go with them. But Rich promised he'd be back to see him soon as he can, bringing him a tent and food and supplies.

Rich expressed his appreciation saying, "Gus, you've taken care of me, saved my life. Come with me. I'll take care of you, I promise. I can give you a happy life in our town. Everyone will love you. Amber and I need you to come with us." The old man Gus shook his head no; tears were in his eyes. He'd been there for years, he didn't know how long. He didn't want to go to back to civilization. He just wanted to die in these beautiful woods, his home. His family who owned the land didn't care about him. No one ever had. But for so long in his prayers he'd asked God to please send him a friend. And by gum, He had. His new friend Rich, and his fine dog Amber. Yep, he had a real friend again and a dog friend too and they'll be back to visit him. Why, maybe one day, he may even *go home with Rich to that place, Sandy-By-the-Sea. It's sounded nice to him there. Yep, maybe one day he'll go.*

Yes, all's well that ends well, the new detective surmises to himself as he heads back. "I'll be like those detectives on TV, solving crimes and missing persons on my travels across the country. I Connor Diamond, will be the best hippy psychic detective ever was!"

Noah reads the end again, loving the story, knowing as he reads the last page what a clever writer his father was. He turns to the acknowledgements, hoping the answer is there somewhere. Why did his dad have the affair? It's here somewhere. Sahara was Tina, but what went down? In the novel they only kissed once, not an affair. And then it falls out; the note card he guessed had been in that bottom drawer for over thirty years, written on flowered purple-violet paper in his mother's beautiful cursive:

> Marshall,
> Your book is wonderful, so creative and thoughtful. It's only now I realize how much I've hurt you and why you left for a while. You put our love in your story. I promise, my darling, that I will never hurt you again. I am so truly sorry. I will only love you forever and ever. For you are the love of my life.
> Josephine

Noah turns to the first page of the book. " For my darling, my Josephine."

Noah looks up. "Francis, now I know. They had problems. My mother had an affair, then he had one with Tina. Maybe Tina had parted ways with Phil. My psychic abilities are akin to Connor's. Phil is twenty years her senior. I'm guessing he thought he was too old for her. Maybe everyone in her family and his thought so too. Dad and Tina had a brief affair and she kept it a secret and so did my parents. Mother forgave Dad and he forgave her. It is a love story, Francis. Their story is a love story of forgiveness and devotion. Thank you."

I say goodbye to Noah. I tell him I'll be near and when it's his time to go, I'll be there. "You have a long life to live, Noah. Now, live it with Maggie, live it with love and forgiveness." It's then I disappear as I see him stand bewildered, not wanting me to leave, but knowing I have to. For humans need to find their own way, make their own decisions with a little angel help along the way.

22

Goodbye

As I slip away from Noah's to my home and take King jogging early, my heart is full of falling into love with Noah. And today? Today is the day...*The Songfest for the Angels*! Keeping my nerves at bay, I try to think positively about my song. My heart bursts in anticipation for the boy who had a dreamy vision of angels, about the miracle of the song they gave him to play for everyone in the world. No one has heard it but Hannah and Reverend Carlos. They say words can't do it justice. July must be an angel. She named her baby Heather Angel. Hannah, Gabe, Chris, January, Taylor, and Josh. They are the angels in town living as humans. It's amazing, wondrous. It's hard to imagine what their true lives are like. Do they fly? How? Where? Are their wings gold like my dream angels or white? I look up at the morning stars with wonder and hope. Does my dream angel know them? Of course he must. Sam Blakely, who wrote the book about Hannah, didn't realize he was right all along. How did they all pull that one off? How did they keep it a secret?

I have practice this morning at eleven with the choir and the quartet. All of Mystic Bay will be engaged in making this the best day ever. The media think it's just *The Songfest* but *The July North Show* will surprise them all. Hopefully, the attention will be on the community center that July spoke about in our meeting. We will raise funds for the AVA Community Center. It's the Angel Vibe Association's community center for the children of Mystic Bay and Riverton. Riverton, southwest of town, is more in need.

The sun is not visible, just a pinkish dawn inching its' way up the sky. Noah will be here soon to jog with his pack. I see Mr. B. walking with a small black dog in his arms. He puts her down and she walks with a limp on the path towards us. King is ready to visit this little sweetheart.

Mr. B. no longer wears his cap, though he wears a Mystic Bay shirt and jeans and his usual sneakers. His white hair tousles in the breeze. A wide grin fills his face. Before I can ask about his dog, he tells me how he heard about *The Songfest TV show* and that I'm singing the tune he whistled the first few days we met. "Maggie, it will be just grand!"

My heart is full, looking at my new friend. "It will be, I know. Mr. B., tell me about your dog here. Did you just get her?"

"This little one is an angel. Seraphina, I named her. Doc Josh said a car hit her and Seraphina needs a home. I hope you will take her. I have to leave after the show for a while. Will you take her to your beautiful life with your Great Grandmother and Gram for me?"

Caught totally off guard, I reply, "Well, well, yes, of course. I'll do anything for you." This is a surprise. Where is he going, I wonder? We can manage one more dog for sure."

"Maggie, you can do anything you set your heart to do. I'll always be here."

"Mr. B," my breath is short. " I don't want you to leave now. I want you to see the Songfest." I pick up the little dog, so fragile, so obviously neglected. I can't help it and start to cry. Why am I crying? I've only known Mr. B. such a short time. But meeting him each day has been comforting for me, a moment in time like having a surrogate father. He spoke gently to me. He came to my rescue with Brian that day and was always here each morning with a whistle and a smile for us.

"Maggie Joy. You were always meant to sing for the angels because of your loving heart, your ability to hear the soul of nature."

How does he know my middle name is Joy? Does he know about the hum? Someone must have told him. Somehow I sense Noah walking this way now. I turn to see him coming down Beach Road with the dogs.

"Don't cry, please. I promise we'll see each other later, Maggie. I will be at the event today...and I will be cheering you onward."

This is surreal, as if a scene from a storybook. The wind is blowing my ponytail now. Sea birds seem to gather around us. I hear the hum of the trees calling me even with the lapping of the morning waves; I hear the sounds of our beautiful life on earth. "But Mr. B., I want you to meet Noah. I've haven't told you about him. He's almost here. See him coming up the road now with all his dogs."

"I know all about Noah. He was in your dream so long ago. Two hearts destined to be together. I have to go, but Sera, now you be good for my Maggie." He kisses her head. Mr. Neal Beasley hands me a white feather. It's like all the white feathers I found around our house. "You are a treasure, Maggie, one in a million," he says as he walks away. "I'll be seeing you and you too, my wonderful King."

Frantic, I turn back to see Noah.

Then I turn back to see Mr. B. turn back and look at me once more. He takes off his glasses; his eyes sparkle golden light, starlight like Josh's, Hannah's, her dad's, like Taylor's and July's, January's and Chris's. He turns back around and wings appear like sunlight dancing on the water...golden and bright like thousands of gold coins. I hear the rustle. I see them shine. Mr. Neal Beasley's my angel! The angel I've been with in my dreams. Then he is gone in a whip of light. There's nothing left where he stood but some glittering gold like someone has thrown golden confetti.

"Mr. B., Mr. B.," I call, running with King by my side and Sera in my arms, but Mr. B is gone. I keep running and running until I hear Noah shouting, "Maggie, what's wrong? Maggie, stop!"

I stop turning back to Noah who is running towards me now with Nursie and Murph in his arms and his other three on the leash. He catches up to me, completely out of breath.

"Maggie, what happened? Why were you running with that little dog?"

I'm crying. "Did you see him? Mr. Beasley? Did you see him?"

"Who? No, Maggie, all I see is you and the dogs."

"Mr. Beasley is my guardian angel. He disappeared. He has golden glowing wings. I saw my angel! I know him like you know your angel, Francis. Neal Beasley was the angel who flew me to see you in the childhood dream!"

The clock tower tolls seven and I feel like I am flying, flying with pure joy.

23

Songfest For The Angels

There's a feeling in the air today, a feeling of complete happiness as July North is introduced. "It's *The July North Show* from the beautiful seaside town of Mystic Bay, California! And here she is, July North!" July sweeps up the bandstand wearing white jeans, jeweled sandals, and a blue tee shirt. Her hair is tied back in a perfect ponytail. Her face is aglow. It's angel's glow, isn't it? For some reason, only I can see it. How extraordinary! I'm the one to see these things now and to keep the quiet knowledge between Noah and me. Angels really live as humans here.

July waves and shouts, **"Hello,"** as she stands next to white whicker chairs on the bandstand, welcoming her viewers and the town. Jumbotrons are set at opposite ends of Main Street, and it's closed to traffic. There are lawn chairs and beach blankets and people old and young with kids and babies in strollers. Some people have brought their dogs. A few media are probably here, but really only the TV crew is evident. Townspeople and tourists line the streets. Many have gone to their rooftops as the Jumbotrons can be seen for over a half mile. On the rooftops of houses and buildings, our neighbors have a great view of the town, the ocean, and the greatest TV Show ever to be seen by millions. Whoever is watching from our country and from around the world will have reactions, but what will they be, I wonder. Will there be epiphanies? Will it bring more hope to the world, more peace, more joy, more love? Will other children see angels? We can only wish it so.

Mayor Willie Walin stands by the other whicker chair and the big show begins. "Welcome, everybody!" July almost sings. The cheering finally calms down. "We're revisiting Mystic Bay, California, the lovely town by the seaside, where people are doing the works of angels. The Angel Vibe Association has done great work, as those of you know who saw my last show here. They're volunteering, fostering children, and adopting those in need. They're helping the homeless and doing good, random acts of kindness. My guest today, the honorable long-time mayor of this fair town is Willie Walin. Welcome Mayor!" July's shiny gold earrings sparkle in the sun. Willie is wearing the town's blue tee-shirt also. There is a large stage built for us to their left where the choir and I, with the San Francisco quartet, will sing and play. A beautiful piano is placed on the stage for Benny. We sit in chairs, also wearing the bight blue tee shirts. Like July, my hair is in a ponytail, as the breeze blows soft and sweet.

Mayor Willie says, "Thank you, July. It's an honor to have you here again. We are truly blessed today. As you know, our town has done wonderful things in the last two years helping others. We are volunteering at shelters in San Francisco, and volunteering here in our fair town, and extending now to the great town of Riverton to the southwest. Rescuing animals in need is a large part of our organization too. It's been life-changing. Everyone in town is on board with the wonderful feeling of giving back to the community. With a large donation from several companies, including other incredible sponsors, we are starting a new community Center, the AVA Community Center, to be located on the edge of town servicing the children and families of both Mystic Bay and Riverton."

"Mayor Willie, this is such wonderful news. The children of both towns will be given free art programs, after-school programs, and weekend activities." As Willie speaks more about the center, July's eyes shine like all angels do.

July introduces us. "We are so pleased to have here the San Francisco Symphony Quartet accompanying the Mystic Bay High School Choir and Maggie Malone, soloist, directed by Carol Sands. They're singing for the angels and for you today, for everyone who is watching us here in Mystic Bay and around the world. Listen, listen to the words of this beautiful song."

The quartet starts the intro of my favorite song. I hear the choir behind me as I sing, "Bless the Beasts and the children. Keep them safe, keep them warm." I want to close my eyes but don't. I see Gram and Tim in their lawn chairs with King by their side. They sit in the front row GG in her wheel chair and Seraphina on her lap. We have all fallen in love at first sight with the little dog and she with us. And who wheeled GG all the way from Moon Road? Why, there he is, Mr. Jamie Bond next to Tim with Emma Rose in his arms. He's smiling too, like so many others. Elena is sitting next to them. It's obvious; they have decided Emma Rose is their priority even thought they are not a couple. I sing my heart out, looking at them. But it's not only the quartet and choir playing and singing with me. I hear other voices sweet and clear. I hear a choir of angels singing with us too. This is like a beautiful dream. Their voices sound sweet beyond description. I look at the crowd of happy faces; many are singing along.

Noah's in the second row with Cal, Lorraine, and his father, who sits in a wheelchair. Noah looks at me and my eyes try to send him the same message of love I feel from his eyes. I look back at GG, Gram, Tim, and King and King turns his head, looking up at the bell tower. He's there perched with Jeb on the roof. Mr. Neal Beasley, my angel, is dressed in his white robe, glittering gold wings by his side. His hand is on Jeb, the dog I will always love. He waves to me and I know he's proud of me. I feel only love and gratitude for my guardian angel. I can really see him and the spirit of my beloved Jeb. Then he is gone in an instant and I sing my solo part now. My eyes look at Gram's eyes. I see joy in them. She so loved the name Joy and it became my middle name, the favorite part of my name. I look at GG and she winks her little wink. The song is over and the applause is thunderous. People are smiling, talking. Did they hear the angels sing too? Maybe they did. I can't wait to tell Noah how I could hear their voices. I think I will tell GG and Gram about the angels. They need to know. I have to share this quiet knowledge of the angels. They really happen to be our friends.

We bow and bow again and the show goes to commercial. People in the crowd are talking and laughing and the whole atmosphere is light and beautiful.

I see Hannah and her family in the first row near Gram and GG. Hannah smiles up at me while her husband Josh, Gabe and Aunt Helen busy themselves with the twins. She waves to me, her eyes shining like star beams. How incredible, I can see them from here.

As the show returns, July asks Willie, "Something has happened in Mystic Bay, am I correct, Willie? Something to do with angels?"

"Yes, July," Willie says with utter calm and sincerity. "We are announcing today that real angels have appeared to three children in Mystic Bay." There is a hush over the crowd; people seem to lean in listening. I look at the Jumbotron as it scans the faces of the crowd. Mayor Willie begins. "The three children are ten and younger. Two of the children have special needs and their names must be kept anonymous. One child spoke for the first time. The child said the word "Angel" the other day. Now this child, a few weeks later, is speaking in little phrases. The angels appeared to another child who has drawn and painted two pieces of artwork at the request of the angels. The miracle is the child could only scribble before. I will show the first drawing done with crayons. Please look at the screen." Up on the screen appears the angel with the dog in his arms. The colors are beautiful like pastel ice crystals. I'm staring at the screen almost in disbelief at the sight. It is so quiet that the only sounds to be heard are the occasional cough in the crowd and the birds singing in the trees. The next painting appears on the screen. Angels are painted representing three ethnicities. And amazingly, both paintings show them singing, singing for the world. The angels have looks of joy on their faces.

July stands, pointing to the Jumbotron. "Many will find this is hard to comprehend, Mayor, and yet here the artwork is for all the world, artwork done by a child. It's a true miracle. This painting looks impressionistic. Amazing angels!"

"Angel," shouts the little voice coming form the hushed crowd. I look at Emma Rose and she is pointing at the big screen. I begin to panic but then Patrick shouts "Angel" too. Miraculously, all the children in the crowd begin a chorus, a chant of "Angel, Angel, Angel." The crowd is on their feet shouting, applauding. Hopefully no one connected Emma Rose or Patrick with the sightings. It doesn't seem so. Seeing Patrick's drawing so large on the screen brings the force of this sighting to everyone, this message to the world. How did he do it they will ask? The answer will be, it's an unknown, a gift from heaven that lasted a moment and was gone like the golden sundown each blessed day.

TO CATCH AN ANGEL

After a minute or two of shouting and cheers, the audience calms down as Mayor Willie speaks again. He stresses how these children must have anonymity and protection, and that the message is clearly for the individual to contemplate.

July asks him his beliefs. She minimizes her role. She is the reporter, not the one to report about the happenings.

"July, to me, this is not about which faith is real. This is about all faiths coming together. Are we here to witness this happening in our lifetime for a purpose? For right now, so much of our world is indeed tormented."

July remarks with a soft glisten in her angel eyes, "The angels must be happy the town is helping others, but do you think they are calling us all to do more?"

"Yes, July. This is what I think. But I am a mere mortal. Only the God all faiths believe in has the answers."

The show goes to commercial break and we all feel the emotion in the crowd. GG and Gram are wiping tears away, as are many others. Noah is talking to his dad who has that far away look on his face again. He then looks at me and I smile. I look up at the roof of the bell tower, but Mr. Neal Beasley is not there with Jeb. And through the hum of the crowds talking, I listen for the trees. I can almost hear them still.

The show returns and July says, "And another beautiful, joyous message from the angels is about to occur. Tell us, Mayor Willie. Tell us the good news."

"Today, Anthony Chen is the violinist who played for us with the San Francisco Symphony Quartet. Anthony has a son named Benny. We must say his name for he will play for us now. People, it is my pleasure to introduce Benny Chen. Angels have come to him in a dream. They have given him the notes to a song for him to play for all of you. This song is for everyone wherever you are. Ladies and gentleman, I present Anthony and Benny Chen!"

Up the stairs, Benny walks to his father. Beside the boy is his service dog, Vinnie. He holds the beautiful golden lab whose steps help guide the way. Mayor Willie decided not to announce the fact that Benny is visually impaired. It's evident. Benny settles at the piano. Anthony steps up with a microphone.

"Hello, everyone. A miracle happened the other night. Benny had a dream, and angels gave him the melody for this song to play for you. Benny is studying piano and is quite good for his age. But nothing prepared us for the song they gave him. As you listen, you'll hear a song, a message for you. The quartet will accompany him. Benny says the angels call it, "Forever Love, Forever Peace." He steps back to his seat at his violin, nods his head, and Benny and the quartet begin. How many people are watching around the world, I can't imagine. I close my eyes, listening to the most beautiful song I've ever heard. The melody takes me away to the clouds. I can picture the angels leaning over Benny as he slept whispering the notes to play. It's as if no one is in the town square but Benny and the quartet playing the song. I feel hope, gladness. As the last few chords are played and the quartet is silent, there is a silence too in the crowd. It's so silent you could almost hear a snowflake fall.

Then Benny gets up and Vinnie gets up too. Benny takes hold of the dog as the audience breaks into roars of clapping and shouting. I see people crying and laughing in pure joy. As Benny takes a bow, the clapping continues with whistles and more cheers.

"Oh, how the children have inspired us," July says to everyone. "This is the most wonderful day I have ever witnessed. Thank you, Benny and the San Francisco Quartet for the most beautiful piece I have ever heard in my life." There are more cheers and applause.

"I have a surprise for all of you. Please look up on the screen. Here is the newly elected President of the United States and his wife, by his side. "Hello everyone, this is a wonderful day for Mystic Bay, California, and for all who are witnessing your show, July. I would like to thank the children who have seen angels. Thank you for the artwork, for the songs. You all are bringing such joy to the world today. Thank you, July, for delivering to us such an inspiring show. And thank you, Mayor Willie Walin, for all your work to put this amazing event together. It is with great pleasure that I announce that the artwork by the child and a recording of Benny's angel song will tour our country and then the world. The exhibits will be at no cost to the public, thanks to an anonymous donor. These children have been given a gift from real angels. My family and I thank you all and say, "God Bless America. WE believe in angels!"

To say the house comes down would be an understatement. The crowd's enthusiasm is top of the charts. As the show comes to a conclusion, we are asked to sing again the beautiful song. As we sing the glorious, " Bless the Beasts and the Children," on this glorious day, I look up at the robin's egg blue sky. I think everyone is looking up, hoping to get a glimpse of an angel.

24

Bees Fill The Yard & August Weddings Bloom

It's Jenny and Jason's big day. Noah and Sue Cero are having a meeting to work on their new book, **The Rescues of Mystic Bay**. But I've just answered the door to a very polite duo, Entomologists, dear old friends of Marshall Greenstreet.. I escort the gentleman outside to the backyard where Gram and Tim and GG sip tea in celebration. You see Gram and Tim ran away to San Francisco last weekend eloping. How happy we are for them. "Wedding Fever," said Tim as he kissed Gram on the cheek when they told us the news. Tim will be living at our house now and GG is ecstatic. "It took you a while, but you finally did it," GG remarked.

"I asked her for years and years and she finally relented," Tim said with a gleam in his eye.

"I was afraid, but no more," Gram said proudly. "With the angels calling, I knew it was the right thing to do. We plan to have a party at the new restaurant in town, Mahoney's Pub. It just opened and will be so much fun, but first we have Jenny's wedding, and the bee men are here."

They will be here for many days researching our yard, for they have found nests of an endangered bee. They will study the topography of our garden and Noah's. How the plants are attracting the bees.

And my winged gold angel bee I captured on my cell phone?

The Entomologists say there is no such species documented anywhere. "It will be a miracle if we find it here," they says emphatically, "but we will search your yard and Noah's. For just as we need to save the trees and forests and seas of our earth, we need to preserve our bee friends to.

"Mystic Bay is becoming quite the nature haven," exclaims Gram.

As sunset comes, I stand in my beautiful shocking pink dress next to Jenny, holding her bouquet of pink roses, as Jason looks lovingly at her sweet face. The beach off Jack's is perfect with the patio for the guests to sit as the couple marries. The reception will be here as the stars come out and the local DJ plays their favorite songs. As she walked up the path, The Angel's Song, "Forever Love Forever Peace" played.

So many things have happened since I moved home to Mystic Bay. I wrote the letter to my mother today, addressing it to Mrs. Lyla Wasserman. I asked her to please tell us about my father if she could. I inquired about her well-being. I asked her to communicate with Gram if possible, how it would mean so much to her. If we get a response, it will be welcome. It felt good to put it in the mailbox at the Post Office, good because it was the right thing to do. If I never get an answer, it will be okay. At least I tried to find the answers. One more try is worth so much.

But right this very second, I think about Jenny's wedding and look over at Noah sitting on the patio next to Tim, Gram, and GG. Ironically, he is very near Tina and Phil. I see him glance at her and then he looks back at me. Then I see her glance at him for a moment. They know they belong to each other now, and the time is drawing near for a meeting. Jenny and Jason promise to each other beautiful vows of love and friendship. After Jenny and Jason walk back up the aisle, we all parade into Jack's By the Sea for a sumptuous wedding feast of clam chowder, pasta and shrimp, wines and salads, I take in the wonder of the family and friends I love so much. I have Mr. B. my angel to thank for coming to me in my dream, giving me hope to start life anew, and find Noah. Then the fantastic, almost unbelievable happening of knowing the little children who see angels, who speak to them, make art for them, and play their sweet song. I can see real angels here living as human beings, spreading their love, their good works with anonymity and hope. Why me, I wonder to myself. Why not me? Hearing the trees, the hum of life has been a gift. How precious our earth is. If I were an astronaut, I wouldn't be able to do the work I was hired to do. I would stare all day at the blue earth and clouds below, waiting for the sight of the aurora borealis.

All these ideas swirl in my mind as Jenny dances with her father and Noah twirls me on the floor. Tim dances with his new bride Gram. Mario sings for the happy couple, an old Italian tune. Tad asks my cousin Marcy to dance and it seems like a romance could bloom. We party till one in the morning and Jenny and Jason leave for the night at The Sea Watch Hotel. Noah and I decide to help the staff clean up after the guests leave. It's fun to put things away and help clear the tables as the kitchen staff cleans. When all is tidy, we go out in the night among the August stars and walk to Dog Beach.

"I love it here in Mystic Bay and I love you more that anything," Noah confesses.

"And I love you too, Noah. It's like a dream and yet it was always meant to be. Isn't it fitting that here in Mystic Bay I would learn the greatest lesson of all? I would learn how to love."

25

Changing Winds Of September

The wind blows hot this hazy summer day in the near empty house in Beverly Hills. Her beautiful face glows with light coming in the window. She looks up at a hopeful sky. Polly Ann's tears roll down her ivory rose cheeks. She looks down at the tear-stained letter from the daughter she doesn't know. My hand sits on her shoulder. In this instant Polly Ann declares, "I will write her back. I"ll tell Maggie, my daughter, the truth. I will not be afraid to ask forgiveness."

You see, as I stand here invisible to her, my wings at my side, she wonders if she's imagining me, that I'm near. The mother and daughter who don't know each other have needed me so. I think maybe now Polly Ann knows finally what I know. Just as the earth needs the sunshine and some rainy days, everyone needs an angel.

26

Shadow On The Moon

There's an eclipse of the moon at midnight, a blood moon they call it. There's no one on the beach but Noah and me. We've brought Smarty, Shadow, and King who play in the dark waves. The little ones are sleeping. Sera's sleeping with Cookie at 20 Moon Road, and Nursie and Murph are at Noah's sleeping like little twins curled in their bed. Dog Beach is aglow with moonlight. Noah and I stop and stare as the shadow begins its way ever so slowly across the moon. I suppose others are in their backyards or at the harbor observing this miracle of the universe, but we wanted to see it with the water glowing moonlight on our favorite beach.

At home, a most wonderful event happened. Gram's expression has lightened. She's happier than I've ever seen her because we received a letter from Lyla Jasmine. She apologized for ignoring us for these long years. She wished us well and said we would hear from her from now on. Her note told us that my father was a foreign exchange student at UCLA. He's from Argentina; Aron Palicio is his name. He has a winery there and she found his address for me. "I'm sorry I never told Aron. It was a brief affair," she wrote. "So here is his address. If you want to contact him, you must do so yourself."

Gram was relieved to get the letter. We all seemed to feel closure, staring at it. Knowing who my father is has brought a sigh of relief. We know full well by the tone of her letter that Lyla does not want us in her life, albeit the occasional note or card, but somehow it doesn't hurt anymore.

Ironically, the day we got the letter we had an afternoon reception at Café Nikos for Gram and Tim. There were garlands of flowers, and we ate Mahoney's Pub's famed desserts, like their crème de menthe cake. Even Jamie Bond said an almost eloquent toast to his newfound boss and friend, Tim, as we sipped champagne! "Way to go Tim. I mean, Congratulations to the happy couple!" Everyone laughed, for Jamie is surely evolving."

I look at the antique engagement ring Noah chose just for me. It's sparkles like the moon on the water. Yes, everything has come together. My life in LA is just a memory, a learning experience. I know now the lemon experiences of life can turn into happy ones, like drinking lemonade on a hot summer day all year long.

And the children? Patrick still likes to draw, though not the impressionist angel masterpieces any longer. He's a wonderful child who loves school and making new friends. His drawings were the Angel's calling to all that would listen. Emma Rose is talking and happy, a delight to teach. She loves pictures of angels and butterflies. Elena has posted them around her room, and I found her a butterfly bedspread with an angel pillow. She was thrilled. Does she still see angels? Yes. One day not long ago as we strolled by the stream near her house, she took my hand and pointed. She announced, "Angel loves yellow butterfly!" And for a moment I saw Jeb near where she pointed. As clear as day, he was sitting as if waiting for me like he used to. His golden fur swept up high again in the afternoon breeze. His eyes were full of happiness and then he was gone.

How amazing that no one in the media got wind of Patrick or Emma Rose's names. And if folks know the story in our fair town, why, they keep it to themselves. That's always been the way here. It's one of the reasons everyone seems to stay. Benny's dad has explained to the press, there will be no interviews until he is over eighteen. The Angel's Song is played over and over by various musicians from weddings to the White House and to countries all over the world. It's a piece that is unforgettable, like the sound of rain falling. The notes can help mend a broken heart or awaken a wishful dream.

"We have company, someone's coming this way, coming fast," Noah says looking down the beach. The background sound of gentle waves gives way to the voices becoming louder now as we look to the south, but can't see anyone. Noah points, "They're coming from the sky!" It's Hannah holding on to Josh's hand as he flies her above the beach. His majestic wings shine like iridescent rainbows caught in the moonlight. They are talking and laughing and don't seem to notice us below.

We stand motionless, not speaking, stunned at the sight. A few moments later, Laurjean and Donnie fly above us. They don't see us either. Donnie's giant wings take them aloft and they call back to the next flying angel, Taylor, whose golden wings shine as he sails towards us. "Hurry, let's catch up to Josh and Hannah," Laurjean calls back to Taylor. Taylor is holding the hand of his lovely wife Hattie, whose face beams with happiness. They are flying together; a flock of angels looking up now, watching the magnificent shadow on the moon begin its' journey. Lastly, July and her sister January fly with milky white wings glowing and little Heather Angel in July's arms. They're wings are mirrors of each other's. July looks down and sees us. She laughs and January looks down and sees us too. January waves their hellos as they soar onwards to catch up with the others flying into the night.

We turn to each other, not really believing what we've witnessed. "Maggie, tell me what you just saw."

"Flying angels, Josh, Donnie, Taylor, July, and January holding their spouses hands and July holding her baby. They're watching the shadow on the moon!"

"Hannah is half angel, just as you thought! This is truly extraordinary, beyond our wildest dreams to see! Look how the dogs are tracking them too. But yet they don't even bark. It's as if the dogs have always seen them!"

"Are we dreaming, Noah? How I wish we could catch their hands and fly along."

"Maggie, I guess we mortals aren't meant to catch an angel, but only fly with them in our dreams like you did when you came to my window. Maybe Francis will take me flying in a dream one day; I'll have to ask him. Yet here we are able to witness this…another miracle in real time, but this time we can't tell anyone, for it's a gift we've been given." He holds me close and we watch them fly far away now, high above the harbor with glowing crystalline heavenly wings becoming tiny specks in the night sky. They're disappearing, dimming like candle light one by one.

The shadow of the moon is moving faster now. We marvel how we know angels living as humans in our picturesque seaside town. They can even fly with their loved ones.

And to think a newfound breed of bee has been sighted in Mystic Bay too. Instead of swarming media, there are swarms of entomologists and environmental groups looking in town, in backyards, especially ours for the bee. The entomologists rented rooms above Dear Dogs, Etc. so they can dedicate their entire work now to finding the elusive bee. What will they name it? They surely will find it, GG and Gram predict.

Noah holds me tight and I close my eyes listening to the sound of the waves. "I want to write, Maggie. I want to write about the bees, and the angel sightings and all I've learned in Mystic Bay. Indeed, it's here we both learned life's most precious lessons…a journey paved by love and angels. And now, I want to tell the story to the world."

27

June Again Once Upon A Time

We chose to marry a year to the day we first met. The sea winds moved east across the ocean like a caress from heaven. Dog Beach was empty but for our small wedding party and the few onlookers with their salty dogs. Reverend Carlos and all who gathered were barefoot. Everyone wore colors that matched the sunset and rainbow colored sky. My dress, Hannah's Aunt Helen's waterfall design, cascaded to a full chiffon skirt at my knees. It was strapless with a lace bodice. Noah, Jason, and Tm wore white pants rolled up and blue Hawaiian shirts. Mabel and Acedro rode GG in a wheel chair on a path made of boards. She wore her favorite purple flowered dress. Gram wore a dress of powder blue, of course. As my maid of honor, Jenny, was delighted to wear the satin pink sheathe Aunt Helen designed as well. Jack and Stella were there too and had the reception all ready for us at the restaurant where all our friends would gather. Tad was in charge of everything. Waiting there would be sour dough bread, vegetarian lasagna, salads, and chocolate cake made with love by Mario and Gor Don.

Tina looked lovely wearing pale yellow lace. Yes, Tina's secret is out now, at least to the family and close friends. Jason was perplexed at first, but now delighted to have a half brother. And it seemed Phil had a moment or too, but the situation seemed to heal itself just as Francis had predicted. Tina told Noah, "At the time, I thought it was the right thing to do. And perhaps it was, for your parents brought you up so well. How can I regret the love you received?" I thought it such a wonderful message for Noah to ponder on later. Lessons learned are gifts to us, aren't they?

Last Christmas, Francis took Noah's father, Marshall, to heaven. Noah said he saw his father's spirit leave with Francis by his side. "Farewell," his father spoke his last words to him. "I'll be seeing you!" Noah was able to tell his father he loved him once more. For you see, as he went to his Maker, Marshall, the clever writer, and Noah's kind father's brilliant mind was renewed once more.

Mr. B. was near at the wedding, but I only caught a glimpse of him for a moment standing behind Reverend Carlos. His wings gleamed golden in the sunset's light. His loving face smiled, yet I saw him wipe a tear from his eyes. Yes, angels really do have tears, for he clearly had tears of joy for me. He

TO CATCH AN ANGEL

left again in a whip of light as a white feather floated to the sand. If anyone noticed me pick it up, they didn't say. I held it as we took our vows. "Forever be my love," we said to each other. In the distance I heard the whistling of a tune. Mr. B. would always be near. I knew that as sure as I knew our love for each other.

We're moon bathing again, sitting on the rooftop of our cozy brown-shingled cottage on majestic Fire Island, watching the sun set over the Long Island sound and the airplanes taking off and landing in a blue and pinkish sky. It's even more beautiful here than Noah described. The deer roam free, no cars, just quiet rustlings and the sounds of the sea. The people here are friendly. It has the angel vibe feel of our little town, our lovely seaside Mystic Bay.

In the past months, the world has been watching and listening and speaking of angels. Some towns and city folk are changing their lives for the better, doing good works for their fellow man, for the animals and for our good earth. July's TV show continues to follow the domino effect of kindness in different places around the country.

The artwork is touring the country. There have been children's sightings of angels in Eastern Europe and the Middle East. Of course, there are skeptics. But will there always be?

Noah and I leave next week for Argentina to meet my father, Aron. He has a wife and son and they are looking forward to meeting me, he told me. What will it be like? I'm not scared, for life has given me a new adventure and Noah will be at my side.

"It's a gift, a process that will take time as love always shows us," predicts GG's ever-escalating wisdom.

Noah reaches for my hand. "Mrs. Greenstreet, can you see those stars coming out one by one now just for us?"

"Yes, how I love it here so very much as you knew I would!" His amber eyes catch the last summer eve's glow.

"Do you think we'll catch angels flying by us tonight?"

"Wouldn't that be wonderful? Do you think they live as humans everywhere in the world, flying at night when no one can see except a few lucky mortals?"

" Yes, I really do," says my husband, the man an angel brought to me.

We sit awhile in silence. Then, the breeze is gone and the sky turns to indigo. The sound of the sea calms us as the last sea birds head home. Then I hear it, a welcome surprise.

"Noah, I hear them."

"What, darling Maggie? Do you hear angel's wings again? Perhaps they've sent us a wedding gift from above."

"Not angels wings, but something I never thought was possible. I can hear the trees here in Fire Island, just like home in Mystic Bay. I can hear them even above the sound of the waves. Their humming is unique, the rhythm moves with the sea. Noah, I can hear it. They're whispering our names!"

Stella's Grandma's Apple Torte

Preheat oven to 350 degrees.
Peel and slice apples half way up. 2 to 2 1/2 big apples placed in greased pie pan.
Shake 1 tb each of cinnamon and sugar on top
On the stove, melt ¾ cup butter on low/medium heat
Add ¾ cup sugar and stir.
Add one cup flour and stir.
Turn off heat and add one egg and stir. Take off heat.
Add touch of milk and stir.
Pour over apples.
Bake 350 for 45 minutes. Serve hot or cold with or without ice cream

Made in the USA
Middletown, DE
26 February 2017